More Stories from The-Front-of-Beyond

© Day One Publications 2023

First printed 2023

ISBN 978-1-84625-739-1

Published by Day One Publications
Ryelands Road, Leominster, HR6 8NZ

TEL 01568 613 740 FAX 01568 611 473

email—sales@dayone.co.uk

UK web site—www.dayone.co.uk

Internal design by **documen**

Cover design by **Kathryn Chedgzoy**

Printed by **4edge**

Dedication

This book is dedicated to Home for Good, a
Christian charity with a Biblical mandate to care
for vulnerable children.
Home for Good is dedicated to finding a home for
every child who needs one.
See homeforgood.org.uk

For those children who are adopted or
fostered, these stories are especially for
you.

Stefan has a choice

Chapter one

Stefan rubbed his fingers in disgust. Another dinosaur's claw had got splodges of jam on it. He hated being sticky. He usually washed the dinosaurs before putting them away, but for some reason he had forgotten to do so.

He didn't like half-term much. February was a boring month. Easter seemed a long way off. Playing pretend beginning-of-the-world games would do. At least it would pass the time.

It had been a long time since Christmas, when he had become a hero for the first time. Solving the dreadful problem of The-Front-of-Beyond giants had been really exciting.

The-Front-of-Beyond. Stefan loved living in The-Font-of-Beyond with Mor and Malc, his foster carers, and Nick, his older foster brother. And there was Mamo as well, the best grandma ever.

Stefan remembered Malc telling him the story about how The-Front-of-Beyond came into being. A long time ago, a king had had a new map of Great Britain made, and he'd put The-Front-of-Beyond next to The-Back-of-Beyond at the top of Scotland because there was a lot of space there ...

The phone downstairs rang. He could hear Mor's footsteps as she went to answer it. He had kept his bedroom door open, hoping that Nick might ring. Nick had gone to a place he couldn't pronounce to see a football ground with Malc. He had never seen one before. He wanted to count the rows of seats before going again to a real match.

Stefan listened. Mor's voice sounded very posh. It couldn't be Nick—she wouldn't have sounded like that.

'Stefan—the phone! It's Mrs Tie-string,' she called out.

He ran down the stairs, leaving the dinosaurs to their fate. You didn't keep an IB, or Important Beyonder, waiting. IBs held very important jobs in The-Front-of-Beyond.

He darted to the phone and took it from Mor. Stefan hoped he had got there in time. Mrs Tie-string, being the post lady in The-Front-of-Beyond, was used to things happening fast.

'Good morning, Mrs Tie-string,' he said in his politest voice.

'Thought you would never come, Stefan. They've gone!'

Stefan didn't think it polite to ask what was gone. It might have sounded rude. He knew Mrs Tie-String kept chickens. A picture of clucking chickens running in all directions down the high street popped into his head. He did his best not to laugh.

'Would you like me to help catch them, Mrs Tie-String?' he asked.

'Catch them! What are you talking about? I want you to find them.'

Stefan was at a lost what to say next. He was now used to being asked for help since the problem with the so-called giants. However, finding chickens—where would he begin? Had they flown away? He didn't know if chickens could fly. Did he dare ask? He took a deep breath and spoke. 'Have they flown away? I mean, do chickens fly, Mrs Tie-String?'

'Chickens no, trainers. They've gone.'

Stefan was now completely lost.

'Should I come round, Mrs Tie-String?'

'Yes, and be quick.'

Stefan put the phone down.

'Got to go, Mor. Mrs Tie-String wants some help,' Stefan called out to Mor, who was now in the kitchen.

'Alright, but wear a warm coat and take some mittens.'

'Yes, Mor,' replied Stefan. He grinned. Mor was being her usual fussy self again.

He found his coat and put it on. The mittens, he knew, were in his coat pockets. He took them out and put them on too. He opened the front door and let himself out.

The post office was in the centre of the village. It was a ten-minute walk from his house. Stefan liked the look of the outside of it. The bright red sign with the words 'Post Office' looked cheerful next to the bright red postbox on the wall. The few climbing plants next to it were red as well. Mrs Tie-String also had red hair. Stefan wasn't sure if her hair was meant to be red as there were some black bits near the top of her head, but the sight of red hair dashing past every house in the morning cheered everyone up.

He knew Mrs Tie-String was a widow and that she was thirty-five. He had heard Mor say it to Mr Right-page once in the library. Stefan didn't know why she said that to him, and he also didn't know what a widow was. At the time he had decided to ask Mor in the library what it was. He had begun to speak, but someone standing near to him whispered 'Shush', so he kept quiet.

At that time he had been learning about spiders at school. There was one called a black widow spider that ate her mate.

He wondered if Mrs Tie-String had eaten her husband! Stefan decided there and then he would be very polite to widows. It was the best way if you wanted to stay alive. He would do his very best to help Mrs Tie-String find whatever was lost.

He began to hurry so much that he almost didn't see Toby across the street.

'Stefan,' called out a cheeky voice, 'over 'ere.'

Stefan stopped and looked across the road. Toby was waving at him.

'Can't stop, got to help Mrs Tie-String. See you later.'

Stefan saw Toby's lips go down. He guessed Toby had no one to play with. Toby hadn't been in The-Front-of-Beyond for very long. Stefan had liked him the minute he joined his class at school. Toby, like Stefan, couldn't spell very well. They became friends really quickly. It was a shame he couldn't stop today.

Stefan arrived at the post office very out of breath. He opened the door and went inside. Mrs Tie-String was behind the counter, counting some money. She was alone. Stefan stood very still, not knowing what to say or do. He saw her lift her head, then without warning jump up when she saw him and dart to the door. She turned the 'Open' sign to the 'Closed' one. He was then hustled towards a door which she opened.

'Stefan, this is where I live. It's a small flat, big enough for me. Off you go then. I've searched the bathroom, the bedroom and the kitchen. I can't spend any more time looking—I need to mix some paint. I want you to search the lounge. When you've found 'em, knock on this door. It's the kitchen. There will be cakes and juice waiting.'

Mrs Tie-String then left the room. Stefan was left feeling very puzzled. He hadn't understood about the paint, and what was he supposed to look for—chickens or trainers? Or had Mrs Tie-String said trainers when she meant chickens?

Maybe if he looked around, he might just see a chicken hiding somewhere out of sight. If he found a pair of trainers instead, that would solve the problem!

Where to begin? He didn't want to be too long in case Mrs Tie-String got cross and decided to eat him. Fortunately an idea came into his mind: start the search in one corner of the room and work his way around. The corner where the television was seemed a good place to begin.

He ran across to where the TV was standing. There was a cupboard underneath it. He opened it. That wasn't good. A pile of books fell onto the floor. He picked them up, noticing that most of them were about chickens! Stefan gathered them up and pushed them back into the cupboard. He closed the door quickly in case they all fell out again and then looked behind the cupboard. Definitely no chickens or trainers.

He then continued his search around the room. He looked behind the settee and even under the cushion! No trainers and happily no chickens. He was relieved about that. The thought of a squashed dead chicken gave him the horrors.

The coffee table was next. He didn't stop as it was clear nothing could be hiding there. He then looked underneath the long curtains at the window—nothing hiding there. He then looked under the armchair cushions and behind the books on the bookcase, still nothing. The fire place was next. He looked behind the coal bucket that was standing next to it. The space was empty.

He had gone around the whole room, running all the time. He stood still to catch his breath. Now what should he do?

There was only one thing he could do—knock on Mrs Tie-String's kitchen door and beg for mercy! He knew it was no good trying to run away.

He could never run as fast as Mrs Tie-String anyway. She could run faster than anyone else, even the strong men in The-Front-of-Beyond. She said it was because of the trainers she always used for delivering the post. At Christmas the only way she could get all the presents to everyone was because of the trainers.

For some reason, she could run faster in them than in anything else she wore on her feet. If these were the ones that were lost, then it was serious.

If it were the chickens that were lost, then that was serious too. Stefan knew Mrs Tie-String loved her chickens. Everyone knew she entered shows for the best chicken. If she won a prize, she would tell everyone she met in the street that she had won.

Stefan took a deep breath and knocked on the door. Immediately it was opened by Mrs Tie-String.

'Found 'em?' she asked.

Stefan still didn't know if he was supposed to be looking for chickens or trainers. As he hadn't seen either, he shook his head.

'Oh, that's bad. I've got boxes to paint as well as the post to deliver.'

This explanation didn't help Stefan much. He couldn't imagine the chickens living in boxes. Neither could he imagine why Mrs Tie-String would want to paint the box that the trainers had come in.

'Sorry,' he said. At least the word sorry was alright for both trainers and chickens.

'Well, I need 'em, but I did say there were cakes and juice waiting, so come and have some.'

Stefan followed Mrs Tie-String into the kitchen. Sure enough, on the kitchen table there was a dish of sticky honey cake with a plate next to it. Standing next to the cake was a large jug of apple juice and an empty glass.

'Sit down, then.'

Stefan did as he was told and sat down. He couldn't face looking at Mrs Tie-String, who sat opposite him. A picture of a large mate-eating spider was crawling through his head. At least if he was to be eaten, he now had been given his last treat. The thought of it didn't cheer him up.

Stefan took a piece from the plate and bit in. His mouth had gone dry, and he found it difficult to swallow. He poured some juice into a glass and put it to his lips. He took a mouthful, trying to swallow both the juice and the cake at the same time. It wasn't a good idea. He choked and ended up coughing into his hand. Mor had always told him that if he needed to cough, he must always put his hand over his mouth.

'Hey, lad, not so fast. You don't want to die, do you?' laughed Mrs Tie-String.

Stefan tried to smile, but the word 'die' froze his mouth. He wasn't having a good day!

'Well, lad, I need those trainers. I can't paint post boxes without 'em. I've got me round to go quick, then it's back to the chickens. Got a show to go in for.'

Stefan tried a smile again, but his mouth wouldn't budge. At least he now knew he was supposed to be looking for Mrs Tie-String's trainers, not her chickens. It didn't help knowing that though. If he was going to die, then it wouldn't be him who would be looking for them.

Stefan thought of his family at home. Mor, Malc and Nick. He thought also of his new friend Toby. Toby was small like him.

He watched Mrs Tie-String help herself to a piece of sticky honey cake. As he watched her eat, he was aware of her moving towards him. The cake went down in three large mouthfuls. She was so close to him now that he could feel her breath on his face.

'You know, Stefan, there's not much on you.'

Was he going to be gulped down quickly too? He closed his eyes and waited for the first bite of the widow spider. Instead Mrs Tie-String spoke.

'Well, Stefan lad, maybe you'd better have your dinner. Go now and come back this afternoon. Can't have you wasting away, can we.'

Stefan didn't have to be told twice. He was out of
the post office and down the street before you could say
postage stamp!

He was glad he could still run fast. In his mind's eye,
he could see Mrs Tie-String turning into a spider and
chasing him with all eight legs. He arrived home out of
breath. He grabbed the front door handle, opened the door
and was in the hall puffing and panting in the hallway
just as Mor was coming out of the kitchen.

'What's the matter with you?' she asked. 'You look like
you've just seen a kelpie.'

Stefan knew what a kelpie was. Mamo would often tell
him and Nick stories about how this ghostly horse would
come out of the deep rivers and streams in Scotland. Given
a choice right now, he wouldn't have minded if a kelpie
had shown up. It was better than being eaten by a spider.

'Not a kelpie, a spider,' he gasped.

'A spider! You! You're not frightened of spiders.'

'Mrs Tie-String.'

'A spider at the post office! It must have been some
spider to make you burst in like that!'

'No, Mrs Tie-String is a spider. You said it. At the
library. She's a widow.'

Stefan wasn't prepared for the loud laugh which came
deep from Mor's throat. She laughed so much, she had to
sit down on the stairs. Stefan stood very still and put his
head down. He didn't like being laughed at.

'Oh, Stefan, don't take it badly. I haven't laughed like
that for a long time. Come and sit next to me.'

Stefan wasn't sure. After all, it was no joke being eaten
by a spider.

'I know, I'm sorry,' said Mor. 'I'm not laughing at you. It's just, well, I needed a laugh today. I woke up with a splitting headache. It's my fault. I thought you knew what a widow was. A widow is someone whose husband has died. It's got nothing to do with spiders.'

Stefan was so relieved at this news that he grinned from ear to ear. How could he be upset at Mor when his life had just been spared!

'Come and get your dinner. Let's forget about spiders.'

The smell of Mor's cooking and a rumbling stomach put all thought of spiders away. He followed Mor into the kitchen. He sat down at the kitchen table. It would be only him and Mor for dinner today. That was good as she might have some ideas about how to find Mrs Tie-String's trainers. Grown-ups were good at that sort of thing.

The table was already set for dinner. He watched as Mor served two generous helpings of beef stew and dumplings onto hot plates.

'Here you are, a good hot meal on a cold day.' She placed one plate in front of him, then got her own.

Stefan could feel his mouth watering. Mor was alright even if she had mixed him up about widows. He picked his knife and fork up and tucked into his dinner. It was everything a dinner should be. If he got married when he grew up, he would marry someone like Mor. Someone who could make good dinners like her.

Pudding was just as good as dinner, chocolate sponge with custard. They both ate their dinner in silence. It was a kind of rule in their house. Talking always came later. Mor then put the kettle on and poured a glassful of milk for him. Stefan decided this was the right time to ask Mor about Mrs Tie-String's trainers.

'Mor, Mrs Tie-String has lost her trainers. She asked me to find them for her.' He thought it better not to mention the chickens.

'Oh, that's what she wanted you for,' said Mor.

'I did my best in looking for them, but I couldn't find them anywhere. She wants me to go back this afternoon.'

'Our Stefan, The-Front-of-Beyond problem solver,' said Mor. 'Giants are one thing, but knowing Mrs Tie-String, her trainers could be anywhere. They could even have been stolen by someone who wants to run very fast.'

Stefan nodded.

'Mrs Tie-String said she needed them because she had post boxes to paint and the post to deliver, then it was back to the chickens. She said she has got a show coming up soon,' said Stefan.

'Oh yes, the championship show. I heard her tell the Reverend Hard-pew at the coffee morning last week.'

Stefan knew Mor looked forward to the weekly coffee morning at church. That was when she found out about things that were happening.

'So what do I do, Mor?'

'Well, first question is, do you want to help?'

Stefan hadn't thought that he had a choice. After all, Mrs Tie-String was an Important Beyonder. It was a bit like doing what his teacher asked him to do at school. You didn't say no. He spent no time thinking his answer.

'I have to, Mor.'

Stefan liked the smile Mor was smiling now. It showed her lovely dimple in her chin.

'You are a good lad, Stefan, but sometimes, well ... Let's just say no one can do everything. I could have a word with Mrs Tie-String, if you like?'

'No, Mor, it has to be me. I can run fast and crawl into small spaces.'

'So you can,' laughed Mor. 'In that case, you can be the first Front-of-Beyond's running detective. But you must take care. I don't want any wobbly turns.'

'I will,' said Stefan crossing his fingers behind his back.

'Mind you do. Right now, I think the best way to begin is to go and see all the IBs first and ask them if they have seen the trainers or anything suspicious. Most of them go into the post office during the week, even just to buy some stamps. Miss Sharp-needle and Mrs Spinning-top are away on holiday, but all the others are here. But first go and tell Mrs Tie-String that's what you're going to do.'

Stefan grinned.

'Thanks, Mor, I will.'

He liked the idea of being a detective. It was an important job. Maybe if he found the trainers he would be a hero again. That would be good. All he had to do now was help Mor wash up, then he could go. He got up and began to clear the table of the dirty pots. Mor then washed them, one at a time. He dried them and put them away. A few minutes later and the job was done. Then he went into the hall and put his coat and shoes on. He was now ready to go out again.

'Before you go, Stefan,' called Mor from the kitchen, 'you must have one of these.'

Stefan walked back to the kitchen to where Mor was standing. In her hand she was holding a notebook and pen. He took them from her and put them in his pocket.

'Come in handy when you are detecting,' she chuckled.

'Thanks, Mor.'

Now it was time for serious work.

Chapter two

Stefan felt much happier walking back to the post office than he had that morning. Now that he knew he wouldn't be eaten, he was ready to be a detective. Even the sun had come out, making a cool day a bit warmer. He arrived at the post office and knocked on the door. The 'Closed' sign hadn't been changed to 'Open'. He wondered if Mrs Tie-String was busy seeing to the chickens. He had to wait a while until Mrs Tie-String opened the door.

'Stefan, they're still missing,' she said, beckoning him in.

Stefan followed her into the living room he had searched that morning.

'Looked outside, no sign of 'em. It's up to you now, lad.'

Stefan took a deep breath and spoke. Seeing Mrs Tie-String again had made him feel a bit nervous. She still reminded him of spiders.

'Mrs Tie-String, Mor says I can be a running detective if I take care, and that the first thing to do is to visit all the—well, important people like you—and ask them if they have seen anything su—sus-pi-kus.' He felt his mouth go dry, and his knees began to knock too.

'Come on, lad, let's sit down. Don't you worry. It's a good idea of yon.'

Stefan obediently followed Mrs Tie-String as she moved towards the settee and sat down. He sat down, a respectful distance from her.

'Now if you start this afternoon, lad, you could manage five visits today and the rest tomorrow.'

'Please, Mrs Tie-String, Mor says Miss Sharp-needle and Mrs Spinning-top are away on holiday, but all the others—I mean, all the other important ...'

'The rest of us are here, you mean.'

'Yes, Mrs Tie-String.'

'That's fine. So four today then and the other three tomorrow.'

'Yes, Mrs Tie-String.'

'Right, off you go then. Watch how you go.'

'Yes, Mrs Tie-String.'

'I'll see you out.'

They both got up, and Stefan followed Mrs Tie-String through the post office to the main door. She then opened it and let him out.

'Good luck, lad.'

'Thank you, Mrs Tie-String.'

He felt his heart miss a beat. It was up to him now. He had to have a plan. That was something he had learned from the giant adventure. He had to fit with four IBs in one afternoon. He knew where they all lived. Everyone in The-Front-of-Beyond knew that. The nearest to the post office was Mr Ready-cash. It made sense to see him first.

He had no time to lose. Stefan sprinted to the bank. He arrived out of breath, opened the door and went in. It was very quiet in the bank, only one customer. He joined the queue and waited his turn.

When his turn came, he asked to see Mr Ready-cash. The lady at the counter asked why he should want to see a bank manager. Stefan said that Mrs Tie-String had sent him. The lady sniffed a bit, got up out of her chair and came to where Stefan was standing. She then told him to follow her and knock on the door that had Mr Ready-cash's name on it. Stefan did so. The lady then left him without a word. Stefan knocked on the door, and a voice called out, 'Come in.' He did so. Mr Ready-cash was seated at a desk in front of him.

'So, Stefan, Mrs Tie-String has sent you. I am a busy man, so sit down and make it quick.'

Stefan noticed one corner of a comic sticking out of a pile of papers on Mr Ready-cash's desk as he sat down. Stefan knew that Mr Ready-cash loved reading comics.

Stefan, like everyone else in The-Front-of-Beyond, knew that Mr Ready-cash had comics in strange places in his house. That was because Mrs Tie-String had seen them when she delivered parcels and Mr Ready-cash asked her to stay for a cup of coffee. Mrs Tie-String had told everyone that the comics were posted to Mr Ready-cash from all over the world, even Japan. Mr Ready-cash told Mrs Tie-String he had no problem reading them. That was because he was able to speak thirty-five languages, including Irish and Welsh!

Stefan wondered if the comic he could see now was in Welsh. Mr Ready-cash quickly straightened his papers and coughed, making Stefan jump.

'Well, Stefan?'

'Mr Ready-cash, please,' Stefan began, 'Mrs Tie-String has lost her trainers, and she has post boxes to paint, and

there is a competition for the chickens, and she wants
me to find them, and Mor says ask all the Important
Beyonders like you, and Mrs Tie-String said it was a good
idea, and as Miss Sharp-needle and Mrs Spinning-top
are away on holiday, it means four visits today and three
tomorrow.'

Stefan stopped, very much out of breath. He noticed a
little smile come on Mr Ready-cash's face. He was relieved
that Mr Ready-cash was happy and not cross.

'Lost her trainers, you say. That's serious. You came
to the right place. And Mor has suggested you ask all of
us, well—yes, as she says. I haven't seen them, but then I
haven't been to the post office for a while. Lots of money—
er—things to do lately.'

Stefan watched as Mr Ready-cash straightened his
papers again. He didn't know what 'money-er things' were,
but it sounded good.

Stefan was now a bit lost for words. Being a detective
wasn't easy!

'Well, Stefan, that means three more today, and that's
a lot of running. You run fast, I have seen you, but we
can't wear out our Front-of-Beyond hero, can we. I tell you
what. I will ring your teacher Miss Sit-up-straight and
Doctor Be-well to ask if they have seen anything. If you
sit outside for a moment, Miss Cady will bring you some
orange juice. She is the lady who brought you in.'

'Yes, Mr Ready-cash.'

Stefan did as he was told. Miss Cady brought him a
glass of orange juice. Stefan said thank you in his best-
behaviour voice. Miss Cady just said 'humph' and went
away again. He waited patiently. Eventually Mr Ready-

cash came out of his office. When Stefan saw him, he stood up.

'Sorry, Stefan, nothing to report. I spoke to them both on the phone, and neither of them has been in the post office for a few weeks now. I suggest you go to the library next and speak to Mr Right-page. He's an observant sort of chap. You might do better there.'

'Thank you, Mr Ready-cash.'

'Goodbye, Stefan, and good luck.'

Outside the bank, Stefan got his notebook and pen out. He wrote down all the names of the IBs and put a cross next to the ones who hadn't seen anything. He put the letters OH next to Miss Sharp-needle's and Mrs Spinning-top's names, which meant 'on holiday'. He felt relieved he didn't have to go to see Miss Sit-up-straight and Doctor Be-well. It would have been a lot of running, even for him. Plenty of time left to go to the library, which was just a ten-minute walk away.

There were only a few people in the library when Stefan entered. Mr Right-page was sitting behind the information desk telling someone where he could find books about birdwatching. Stefan waited his turn. Then the man went. It was Stefan's turn to speak.

'Good afternoon, Mr Right-page,' said Stefan. Mor had told him to say that to Mr Right-page because Mr Right-page liked good old-fashioned manners.

'Ah, Stefan,' said Mr Right-page, 'how can I help you? Speak clearly now.'

'Mr Right-page, sir,' Stefan whispered, 'Mrs Tie-String has lost her trainers. She has to paint boxes and there is a competition for them. I mean, the chickens.'

'What did you say, a competition for trainers? Speak up, lad.'

'Yes, sorry, Mr Right-page, sir,' said Stefan in a louder voice. Two people both said 'Hush' to him at the same time.

'I mean, Mrs Tie-String wants me to find the trainers because they are lost. Mor told me to ask all the Important Beyonders like you to see if you had seen them.'

'Ah, a good idea. Can't have lost IBs. You have a good luck for them.'

'Yes, um, thank you, Mr Right-page.'

'Sorry not to be of any help, got a library to run, but you is a good sort of chap. If anyone can find them, you can.'

Stefan gave it up as a bad job. He couldn't imagine Mr Right-page pinching Mrs Tie-String's trainers anyway. He was too deaf to be able to run. You can't run if you can't hear as you might get run over. He thanked Mr Right-page again and left the library.

Once Stefan was outside, he took out his notebook and crossed out all the people he had seen. It seemed a sensible thing to do rather than putting crosses beside the names. It meant he could now see the names of the three IB's who were left: the Reverend Hard-pew, Mr Wind-sprout and Mr Spit-it-out. He would visit them tomorrow.

···

The next day, Stefan set out to interview The Reverend Hard-pew, who was the first of the three IBs left on his list. Stefan thought it would be best to visit him first as he was a vicar. Vicars know lots of people.

The Reverend Hard-pew lived in the vicarage, which was a little way out of The-Front-of-Beyond down a small country lane. It was the longest run Stefan had done, and he arrived at the vicarage very out of breath.

The Reverend Hard-pew was expecting him as Mor had rung earlier to make an appointment. Mor told him he had to be extra polite as he would be talking to a man of the cloth. Stefan didn't know what that was. He didn't have time to ask Mor as she was going to see Mamo about something important. He wondered if The Reverend Hard-pew made his own clothes.

Stefan rang the vicarage door bell. He could hear it echoing down the hall. After a few minutes of waiting, Mrs Gillespie, The Reverend Hard-pew's housekeeper, opened the door. When she saw Stefan, she smiled.

'Come on in, Stefan. Reverend Hard-pew is in his study.'

Stefan did so and followed Mrs Gillespie to the study. She knocked on the door and went in. The Reverend Hard-pew was sitting behind his desk.

'Stefan to see you, Reverend Hard-pew,' Mrs Gillespie announced.

'Come in, Stefan, sit here,' said the Reveredn Hard-pew. 'Your mother said it was important.'

Stefan sat down on the chair he was told to sit on, which was opposite the Reverend Hard-pew.

'Shall I stay, Vicar?' asked Mrs Gillespie.

'Oh yes, just in case this young man needs, well, um, help. Nothing wrong, I hope?' asked the Reverend Hard-pew.

'Excuse me, Mr—er—Reverend Hard-pew, sir, but Mrs Tie-String has lost her trainers. She has to paint boxes, and she is very busy with the chickens who are laying eggs, and they will hatch them, and there is a competition for them.' Stefan now knew his speech off by heart.

'Really. Oh, that is serious,' said Reverend Hard-pew.

'Yes, sir, and Mrs Tie-String wants me to find them, and I have asked everyone important because Mrs Tie-String said it was a good idea, and Miss Sharp-needle and Mrs Spinning-top are away on holiday, and I have to ask you, sir, and Mr Wind-sprout and Mr Spit-it-out because they are left on my list.'

Stefan felt proud of his speech. It was much better than yesterday's, and he was not nearly so much out of breath.

Reverend Hard-pew rubbed his chin.

'I wish I could help you, Stefan, but I have been very busy lately. What with illnesses, mainly old people, and—well, you're young. You've got years ahead of you.'

Stefan smiled his best church smile. It seemed the most polite thing to do.

'Oh, just remembered,' continued Reverend Hard-pew. 'I was in the post office last Saturday buying some large envelopes and some stamps. I had an important letter to post to the bishop at the time. There was a long queue, but that's all, nothing unusual happened. I came home then. That's all.'

Stefan smiled again, but it was just a face smile. Inside he was feeling fed up. He was getting nowhere with all the detecting he was doing.

'Thank you, Mr Reverend Hard-pew, sir. Thank you for seeing me. Goodbye.'

'Goodbye, Stefan. Give my regards to your mother. Mrs Gillespie will see you out.'

Stefan got up, walked to the study door and opened it. Mrs Gillespie then saw him out.

Once outside, Stefan crossed the Reverend Hard-pew off his list. He would go and see Mr Wind-sprout next and Mr Spit-it-out last. That was because he had been frightened of going to the dentist since last year. Mr Spit-it-out had told him he needed to take a tooth out because of overcrowding. Stefan had no idea what overcrowding meant. Mr Spit-it-out said it in a very serious voice, and Stefan had never forgotten it.

Stefan liked Mr Wind-sprout very much. He was round and jolly with a ginger moustache that curled upwards. Mr Wind-sprout loved pears. He ate a pear every day. One day when Stefan came into the shop to buy some potatoes for Mor, Mr Wind-sprout gave him some pears to eat. He made Stefan promise to eat one a day for the next week.

He said that pears were good because they had anthocyanins in them. Stefan tried repeating the word, but it came out as 'anso-sinning'. Mr Wind-sprout said never mind the word because anthocyanins helped people to run fast. Stefan believed it was eating the pears that had made him a good runner. Yes, he liked Mr Wind-sprout a lot.

It was a long run back into the village again. When he arrived, Mr Wind-sprout was serving an old gentleman with some carrots, an onion and two potatoes. Stefan waited patiently as Mr Wind-sprout put them into a brown paper bag. He then handed them to the old gentleman.

'There you are, James, with a bit of scrag-end of mutton and long slow cooking, you've got a tasty stew. It'll keep the coughs away.'

They both laughed together. Then the gentleman turned and walked away.

'Hello, Stefan. Mor sent you to buy more parsnips then? She said the other day she has been making soup.'

Stefan took a big breath and began.

'Not soup, Mr Wind-sprout, sir, trainers! Mrs Tie-String has lost her trainers. She has to paint boxes, and she is very busy with the chickens, and there is a competition for them, and Mrs Tie-String wants me to find them, and I have asked everyone important because Mrs Tie-String said it was a good idea, and Miss Sharp-needle and Mrs Spinning-top are away on holiday, and I have to ask you, sir, and Mr Spit-it-out because he is the last one on my list.'

Stefan then stopped. He had said it all in one go, and his heart was beating very fast.

'Trainers, you say. Not seen them myself, but haven't been to the post office in a long time. Don't get many letters ... but then nice to have friends, ones like Mor, such a lovely lady.'

Stefan saw Mr Wind-sprout's smile go for a moment. Then it came back. He grinned at Stefan and spoke again. 'You had better sit down, Stefan, and have a pear. All that running has done you in.' He picked one up. 'Here you are, a nice juicy one.'

Stefan took the pear and thanked Mr Wind-sprout.

'And when you have finished that, you can come and meet Ben.'

Stefan had no idea who Ben was. He tried a polite 'That would be nice' but ended up choking and spluttering bits of pear everywhere.

Mr Wind-sprout patted his back.

'Better now? I tell you what—come back in an hour after you have seen Mr Spit-it-out and we can have a bit of lunch together. Aunty is coming. She's having her hair done. I'll ring your Mor. She can come too. Make a nice treat, it will, for Aunty.'

Stefan swallowed his last mouthful of pear.

'Thank you, Mr Wind-sprout, sir. And thank you for the pear.'

Stefan's heart fell. It was now time to see the last IB on his list, Mr Spit-it-out. There was no getting out of it. Mr Spit-it-out might have a clue. Stefan was desperate for clues, anything at all, even a tiny one.

He said a polite goodbye to Mr Wind-sprout and started off for the dentist's. It wasn't far to go, so he walked there. He arrived about ten minutes later, opened the door and went in. The first thing Stefan noticed was the smell. It made him feel a bit sick.

Swallowing hard, he made his way to the receptionist's desk and waited. The receptionist was on the phone. He was beginning to think it had been a mistake eating the pear. The taste of it was coming back into his mouth. He swallowed even harder this time.

He heard the receptionist say, 'Ten o'clock tomorrow.'
Then she put the phone down and smiled.

'Oh, it's Stefan. Toothache is it?'

'No, er, well, can I see Mr Spit-it-out please? It's
important.'

'Possibly, but you will have to wait. He has a patient at
the moment. I'll pop in when he is free.'

'Thank you.'

Stefan noticed there were two other patients waiting.
He sighed and sat down on a vacant chair. It might be a
long wait. He found a comic in a pile of magazines and
began to read.

He tried his best to read his comic, but his mind
couldn't take the words in. The sick feeling was getting
worse. Mr Spit-it-out's door opened. A lady carrying a
large bag with the words 'Live and let die' written on
it came out. At that moment, Stefan would have gladly
chosen the 'let die' bit. The receptionist got up and went
inside. She came out a few minutes later and went back to
her desk without saying anything.

One of the waiting patients was called, an elderly
gentleman. Stefan watched as he shuffled to the door and
went inside. The door closed. About ten minutes passed
by. Then the old man came out. The next patient, a young
lad with long hair in a ponytail, was called. He sprang
up out of his chair and went in. Eventually he came out.
Stefan thought he looked very pale. The receptionist then
looked up.

'You can go in now, Stefan.'

He took a good deep breath and went in. He was determined to make this a short visit. Mr Spit-it-out gave a broad, very white smile.

'Let me guess, problems with overcrowding again. Sit down and let me take a look,' he said. Stefan was determined not to do anything of the sort. He remained standing where he was. This was going to be short. He began his now-familiar lost trainers speech and ended with, 'Have you seen them, sir?'

'No, I haven't, but while you're here let me see if you have been cleaning your teeth properly.'

Stefan had no intentions of doing anything of the sort. He made a dash for the door, opened it and darted through the waiting room towards the door leading onto the street. He opened it and then began to run away from the dentist's as fast as his legs would carry him.

He arrived back at Mr Wind-sprout's shop in no time. Stopping to catch his breath, he opened the door and went in.

'Stefan, is that you?' Mr Wind-sprout's voice came from the open door at the back of the shop.

Stefan managed a gasped 'Yes'.

'Come on through then, sandwiches and honey cake waiting. Morag's brought some of her best elderberry juice. Lock the shop door on your way, will you?'

Stefan turned and locked the door. He stood still for a few moments to get his breath back. He then walked through the shop as calmly as he possibly could. His mother was there and another lady too whom Stefan took to be Mr Wind-sprout's Aunty. They were all sitting at a small table.

'Well, I never. You walked straight past him. You didn't notice, did you,' said Mr Wind-sprout. 'Now just turn around and look in that corner.'

Stefan was at a loss to know what Mr Wind-sprout was talking about, but he turned around all the same. In the corner was a basket.

'Well, don't just stand there. Go and look for yourself.'

Stefan did so. Inside the basket was a small puppy curled up. It was fast asleep. Now he knew who Ben was. Ben was a dog. It was the best puppy he had ever seen in his life.

'It's alright. You can stroke him, but be gentle. Don't wake him up,' said Mr Wind-sprout.

Stefan tiptoed up to the sleeping puppy, bent down and gently stroked its soft fur. It was magic.

'Got him a week ago, but you come and have your sandwiches and I will tell you all about him,' said Mr Wind-sprout. Stefan came back to the table and sat down next to Mor.

'Wash your hands, Stefan, over there, look,' she said.

Stefan walked to the sink, washed his hands and dried them on a towel. He then came back to the table and sat down again.

'This is very kind of you, Mr Wind-sprout,' Mor said.

'My pleasure. It's not every day I have company. Stefan, this in my Aunty Margaret.'

Stefan had been told that he had to shake hands when he was introduced to a grown-up. He did so now.

Aunty Margaret laughed. Stefan thought it was a nice laugh.

'Right, everyone, let's eat,' said Mr Wind-sprout.Mr Wind-sprout, with Mor's help, brought the food and juice to the table.

'Come on, lad, tuck in.'

Stefan did so. He tucked in his sandwiches and honey cake, relieved that he had escaped from Mr Spit-it-out. For a few minutes, the trainers were forgotten about. Who cared if he had overcrowding. He could still eat.

Chapter three

Stefan could not sleep. He had enjoyed his lunch very much as well as meeting Ben. Mr Wind-sprout had even said he could take Ben for a walk tomorrow. But despite everything he had done, he hadn't found Mrs Tie-String's trainers. The relief of escaping the dentist had lasted for a while, but now it had gone.

He felt bad about himself. He had been given an important job to do, and he had failed. Mor had said she would let Mrs Tie-String know. Mrs Tie-String had said, 'Tell Stefan he did his best.' Mor had said so too. Malc and Nick, who were now home and had heard all about it, said so too.

It didn't make any difference. After all, he had solved the problem of the giants. He was good at running. He wanted to be good at detecting too. He wanted to be good at lots and lots of things.

Were all the IBs telling the truth? Horror of horrors, supposing one of them wasn't telling the truth. He couldn't go back and question them all again. After all, he was just a kid and they were grown-ups and very important.

What he needed now was a new plan.

He tried to think, but nothing came to his mind. He thought a bit more. Then an idea came into his head. Maybe if he could ask Mrs Tie-String to have a meeting in the village hall like they did for the giants. Then she could ask all the IBs herself if they had seen the trainers or anything sus-pi-kus. And then she could ask all the other Beyonders who came the same question. At least she was a grown-up. And he would look after the chickens while she was away. It would be a quick meeting, no cake at the end. In that way, Mrs Tie-String could get back to the chickens.

It might be that someone might know something. And if someone did and confessed to Mrs Tie-String, she would tell Stefan his plan had worked. He would then be a hero again.

That was better. He could go to sleep now.

···

'Mor, can I take Ben for a walk now?'

Stefan had just finished his breakfast. Nick, who was now twelve, had gone upstairs to do his homework. Malc had gone to work earlier on that morning. It was only Stefan and Mor left in the kitchen.

'Yes, but I don't want you running today. A walk is a walk, no funny turns, right?'

'I haven't had a funny turn for ages, since all that stuff with the giants,' said Stefan, putting on his best smile.

'I know, but ...'

A knock on the front door stopped Mor from finishing what she was going to say. She went to answer it.

'Come on in, Toby. He's just finished his breakfast.'

Stefan, who had heard his friend speaking, dashed into the hall. He then grabbed his coat, put on his shoes and was out of the door before Mor could change her mind. He finished buttoning his coat up outside.

'What's the rush?' asked Toby.

'Mor was about to do her "Do be careful" speech.'

The front door opened behind them. They both turned around. Mor was standing there.

Oh no, was he going to be told off, and in front of Toby too? He noticed she was holding a small bag in her hand.

'You can take this to Mr Wind-sprout,' she said. 'It's some of my parsnip soup. And walk. Don't you run. You make sure he does, Toby, and carry this carefully. Jars can break.'

Stefan grinned and took the bag.

'Yes, Mor, thanks.'

The door closed behind them.

'Yer were lucky there,' said Toby.

'No, she gave me the soup to take so that I would have to walk. She usually takes it round herself, but it doesn't matter. Once we've got rid of the soup, we can have Ben.'

'Ben, who's Ben?' asked Toby.

'Mr Wind-sprout's new puppy. We're taking it for a walk, and then we have to go and see Mrs Tie-String.'

'Mrs Tie-String, why?'

Stefan noticed Toby had gone a bit pale. He wondered if Toby also thought that she was a widow spider.

'Tell you on the way, and she's alright, you know, Mrs Tie-String. She's alright.'

'Yeah, well, but ... I 'ad a puppy once,' said Toby as they set off. 'He was ...'

...

They arrived at Mr Wind-sprout's shop a quarter of an hour later. Stefan had heard all about Toby's puppy, which had done extraordinary things and lived a very long life. Toby had also shown him his collection of marbles. He was proud of them. They filled his pocket to the top. Stefan had thought them alright. There was one he liked a lot though. It was red and orange and shadowy like the planet Mars.

Unfortunately, Toby talked so much that Stefan only had a few minutes left to tell him about Mrs Tie-String's trainers. He had just finished when they walked into the shop.

Mr Wind-sprout was busy serving a customer. They waited until she had gone. Stefan then put the soup on the counter. Mr Wind-sprout took the jar and hugged it to his chest.

'Parsnip soup and still warm,' said Mr Wind-sprout. Toby sniggered. Stefan gave Toby's foot a sideways kick. 'Good lad, Stefan, for bringing it. Thank your mother for me. And this must be your new friend.'

'Yes, thank you, Mr Wind-sprout, sir. This is Toby.'

'Toby, yes, nice to have some new Beyonders, and you have a good friend in Stefan, quite the hero.'

Toby didn't answer. Stefan wondered if it was too slushy for him, a bit like Mor with all her fussing.

'Guess you've come for Ben,' continued Mr Wind-sprout. 'Come through, both of you.'

Both boys followed Mr Wind-sprout through the shop. Ben was in his basket, curled up the same as the first time Stefan had seen him. Like before, he bent down and stroked him. Then he stood back to let Toby have a turn. Toby did the same, stroking his back from head to tail, then again and again. Stefan watched his friend. Toby was in another world.

'Well, Stefan, your new friend likes dogs,' Mr Wind-sprout said.

Toby stood up. Stefan saw a small tear on his face and watched as he wiped it away with the back of his arm.

'He's like our Snap, but he's dead, 'said Toby.

Stefan guessed Snap was the puppy Toby had been talking about earlier. For a moment no one spoke.

'Right then, lads, come on. Ben's very much alive, and he'll need to wee. He always does on his walk.' Mr Wind-sprout chuckled. Both lads grinned. Everyone felt better. 'I'll get his lead. He hears me, you know. The minute I open that cupboard where his lead is, he's awake and ready for the off.'

Mr Wind-sprout went to the cupboard and opened the door. Sure enough, Ben was up and barking.

'Told you, didn't I. Look at him raring to go.'

In no time Ben had his lead on and both lads were out of the shop, Stefan holding the lead. They turned in the direction of the park. It was just the right place to go, plenty of open spaces and enough trees for Ben to wee behind.

'Is it alright to let him off his lead?' asked Stefan when they arrived at the park.

'Dunno. He might run off and get lost. Snap did sometimes,' said Toby.

'Oh right. Anyway, he's liking to sniff at things.'

'Yep, best let him do what he wants.'

Stefan couldn't help notice his friend was looking unhappy. Maybe he was missing Snap. Had Snap died a horrible death?

Ben wasn't unhappy though; he was definitely a happy puppy. Sometimes bounding ahead, sometimes stopping to smell something in the grass, Ben was definitely in charge. Stefan and Toby let him lead the way. The dog took them away from the park area and towards some spare land, which was thick with different sorts of bushes.

He stopped at a few of them, smelling all around them until he found one which was just right for weeing against. Stefan turned his head away.

'Doesn't seem polite to look,' said Stefan.

Toby shrugged his shoulders.

Ben was off once more, leading them into longer grass with fewer trees. Sometimes he would bark at little creatures and do a strange dance around them. Then he would lose interest and be off again. He was slowing down a bit now. Stefan looked at his watch.

'Has he had enough?'

But before Toby had time to reply, Ben suddenly darted off.

'Now what's he seen?' asked Stefan, who was now being pulled by a very excited Ben.

'What he's smelled more like ... could be a rabbit?'

Ben was now pulling at his lead towards a group of trees at the edge of the park. Stefan had no choice but to follow, Toby coming behind. Suddenly Ben stopped. Stefan nearly lost his balance and almost fell over him. Ben started pawing and scratching at the ground, which was thick with long grass, weeds and mounds of earth. He began to dig at a furious pace.

' 'Spect it's a dead rabbit. Don't look, could be narsty,' said Toby.

Stefan turned his head away and closed his eyes. He really didn't want to see a dead rabbit, especially if it had creepy things crawling all over it.

'You can open yer eyes now. It's not a rabbit,' said Toby.

'Is it dead or alive?'

'No, none of 'em.'

Stefan opened his eyes and gasped. In his mouth, Ben was a holding something with very dirty laces. It was covered in mud and grass stains. He looked closely at it. Could it be what he thought it was?

Chapter four

'What do we reckon on this being one of Mrs Tie-String's trainers then?' said Stefan as he bent down and took a closer look. He was feeling excited.

'Could be,' replied Toby. 'But thar's only one.'

'Maybe there's another one buried somewhere around here.' Stefan stood up. 'But I don't know why they are here in the park. Still, we have to look.'

Toby was now looking worried.

'It might not be Mrs Tie-String's. It might belong to some kid and he just threw it away.'

Stefan was puzzled.

'Why would someone do that?'

'That's easy—to get some new ones,' said Toby. 'Yer know, he could've said that some kid bullied him in the park and that the kid knocked 'im down and took one of his trainers and threw it away.'

Stefan stared at Toby. He had never heard of such a thing happening in The-Front-of-Beyond.

'Anyway, I've got to go now 'cos it's an early dinner today. Ma is going somewhere, can't remember where,' said Toby.

'Oh, have you? You didn't say,' said Stefan.

'Yeah, well, see yer round,' said Toby.

'Right then, if you have to go, see you later,' replied Stefan.

And that was it. Stefan watched as Toby walked away. Back the way they had come. The early excitement of finding the trainer had gone. What to do now?

Stefan felt let down. Why hadn't Toby said before that he had to be home early? Was he frightened of going to see Mrs Tie-String? He had talked so much about his dog on the way to see Mr Wind-sprout that he hadn't given him a chance to say that Mrs Tie-String was alright and that she didn't eat people.

There was nothing for it. He would have to search for the other trainer by himself. He hoped Ben might help him.

By now Ben was having a happy time chewing the laces on the trainer, which he had now just dropped on the ground.

'Come on then, Ben. It's just you and me now.'

It took a while before they could move off together. Ben would not leave the laces alone. Stefan had to pull the trainer away from him with Ben jumping on the laces as they went. Stefan then had a good search of the area. He looked for quite a while but found nothing. He felt very disappointed. There was only one thing for it. He would have go back to Mr Wind-sprout's and then take the one trainer to Mrs Tie-String.

He arrived at the shop feeling very tired but relieved. Nothing worse had happened to him. He looked through the shop window. He could see there were three customers waiting to be served. He waited patiently until Mr Wind-sprout had finished serving them. He then opened the door and went inside. Ben was now trotting quietly at his side.

'Stefan, you're' back. Better come straight through with Ben.'

Stefan followed Mr Wind-sprout to the back of the shop. Mr Wind-sprout bent down and took Ben's lead off. Ben went straight to his basket and settled down.

'You look all in, lad. Sit down. Has Ben been tiring you out, and where is your young friend? And if I'm not mistaken, that's a trainer in your hand.'

Stefan pulled a chair out and sat down at the kitchen table. Mr Wind-sprout did the same. Stefan then told Mr Wind-sprout about what had happened that morning. He left nothing out. He noticed the smile went off Mr Wind-sprout's face at the bit about Toby suddenly having to go home.

'Well, I don't know what to think about Toby suddenly leaving, and of course the trainer could belong to Mrs Tie-String, but then where's the other one?' pondered Mr Wind-sprout. 'Ben's always digging things up. Mind you, if it is her trainer, then she's run past the shop plenty of times. Maybe Ben recognised it by the smell.'

Stefan sighed. He had no idea what to say or do next. He was feeling very tired too.

'Anyway, as I say', continued Mr Wind-sprout, 'you look all in. Put your arms on the table and rest your head on them. Close your eyes if you want to. I'll see to everything.'

Stefan did as he was told. It was quiet in the shop. All he could hear was Ben making little doggy snores. After a while even those went away.

...

Stefan came to with a sudden jerk. It was Mor's voice speaking. Her head was close to his, and she was whispering into his ear.

'Stefan, it's me. Now just sit up gently. I know what's happened. Mr Wind-sprout rang me up when you were asleep to tell me, and he's rung Mrs Tie-String too. Tell you all about it at home after a bit of lunch. Then it's a quiet afternoon for you.'

Stefan got up out of his chair. There was nothing for it but to do what Mor said. He felt sad. The day wasn't turning out as he wanted it to be. He said thank you to Mr Wind-sprout for letting him take Ben for a walk.

'Look after yourself, Stefan, and if you want to take Ben for a walk anytime, that's fine with me.'

Stefan thanked Mr Wind-sprout again and followed Mor out to the car. Neither of them spoke on the way home. At least he knew when he got home there would be something nice cooking in the oven. There always was. Sure enough, the moment Mor opened the front door of their house, the inviting smell of something meaty snuggled around his nose.

'Chicken casserole with cheesy dumplings,' said Mor.

Stefan grinned in spite of himself. It was his favourite.

'Just you and me today. Nick's at Mamo's. I gave him some of my soup to take, and Malc's got a work meeting. They can have their share tonight.'

'Smells great, Mor.'

The thought of a good dinner cheered Stefan up a bit. He was now feeling hungry.

'Hang your coat up and wash your hands,' said Mor. 'Then come and help set the table.'

Stefan did so.

Stefan then watched as Mor took the casserole out of the oven. She doled out one helping of chicken casserole onto each of two plates, complete with two cheesy dumplings.

'Now eat up, and no talking until we've both finished.'

Stefan began his meal. Every mouthful warmed his stomach. Dinner was followed by a slice of warm apple cake and a mug of tea. Afterwards they cleared the table, washed up and put everything away.

'Right, better now?' asked Mor.

Stefan grinned and nodded at the same time. Mor laughed.

'Food might not be the answer to everything, but it helps. Now how about we both go and sit in the lounge. I'll tell you what Mrs Tie-String said.'

Stefan took the hint. He followed Mor into the lounge and sat down next to her on the settee.

His heart missed a beat. Would Mrs Tie-String be cross because he hadn't been to see her that morning? And what about the trainer? Did it belong to her?

'Look, Stefan,' Mor began, 'I know you want to know about the trainer, so I'll tell you straight. It doesn't belong to Mrs Tie-String. Mr Wind-sprout rang her up when you were asleep. He described the trainer to her. She said it definitely wasn't hers as her trainers have an upsidedown red V pattern on both sides.'

'Oh,' said Stefan, 'Toby must have been right then.'

He then told Mor everything Toby had said about some kid wanting new trainers.

'It could be,' said Mor. 'Mrs Tie-String said to tell you not to worry as Mr Right-page has offered to close the library and paint the post boxes. It means she doesn't have to leave the chickens alone in case someone nasty pinches one of them.'

'But it's not fair, Mor. I was going to say to Mrs Tie-String that she could have a meeting in the town hall like we did about the giants with all the IBs. Then she could ask all the Beyonders who came if anyone had seen her trainers.'

'But Stefan, I've told you before—you can't make it alright all the time.'

'But I have to, Mor. If I don't find them, Mrs Tie-String won't be able to run fast, and we won't get all the nice different presents at Christmas.'

'Stefan, listen to me.'

'No, I won't. You don't understand. You're not my mother anyway.'

He jumped up and ran out of the room.

Chapter five

Stefan didn't like the quietness in the house. He had lain on his bed, thumping his pillow for what seemed ages. After being naughty and running upstairs, he expected Mor to come and tell him they couldn't keep him anymore, but she hadn't. Then he thought she might leave him in his bedroom without any meals for a whole week.

Then he got really scared. Maybe she had gone to get a policeman to arrest him and take him to prison. People in prison didn't have nice food; they only had bread and water. But then he hadn't heard her go out.

But it was far too quiet in the house. Maybe he should go downstairs, but what if Mor was crying? He never knew what to do when people cried. Perhaps if he just opened his door a little bit and listened, it would give him a clue what to do next.

He got off his bed and tiptoed to the door. He opened it very slowly. He didn't want to make a sound. He stood there listening. The house was still, no sounds at all, nothing he could name like the sound of the kettle boiling or the sound of Mor humming. She often hummed. Usually they were Scottish folk songs, the ones they would dance to at Christmas. Maybe she had gone to sleep. She did that sometimes in the afternoon.

Should he go downstairs or stay in his room? He stood
for a while wondering which to do. Nothing came into
his mind, so he closed the door. Maybe if he lay down, he
might go to sleep and never wake up. That was the best
way. He felt tired, so very tired ...

...

'Stefan, wake up. It's me.'

Nick's sudden voice made Stefan wake up with a start.
For a few moments, he couldn't remember why he was
lying on top of his bed.

'Nick?'

Then he remembered everything that had happened.

'Mor sent me up with this, and she wants to know if
you want a drink,' said Nick.

'Did she say anything else? I mean, anything about me,'
said Stefan. He swung his legs out of bed and looked out of
the window, suddenly worried about what Nick might say
next.

'No, why?'

Stefan then told Nick what had happened earlier.

'So that's why she looked a bit sad,' said Nick. 'She
wants you to have this too. She said it's important.'

Stefan looked at his brother. It wasn't sounding good.

Nick then put his hand into his trouser pocket and took
out a neatly folded piece of paper. He handed it to Stefan.
Stefan took it but didn't open it.

'Is it the bill?' he asked.

'What bill?' said Nick.

'Well, before I go, does she want me to pay for all the food I've eaten?'

'She didn't say anything to me about food. Are you going somewhere then?'

'No, yes, well, it depends if she says I have to. I don't like the idea of prison though,' said Stefan, looking down at his feet.

'She said nothing to me about prison, only to tell you to have a good think. Better open it,' said Nick.

There was nothing for it. If it was a bill, he would take it like a man. It was a saying Malc used sometimes.

He slowly unfolded the paper. It wasn't a bill, and there was nothing about prison. It was a picture.

He knew immediately it was one Mor had drawn. She was good at drawing. She had once told him she had worked doing drawings for a newspaper. So that was why it had been so quiet in the house.

The drawing had the five of them on it: Mor, Malc, Mamo, Nick and himself. At the bottom of the picture were five pieces of string, each one next to a person in the family. The strings dangled down the page. The ends of all the strings were knotted together.

Stefan looked at the picture. He had been told to have a good think. So he did. It was easy. The picture said they were one family all joined together, and he was a part of it. He showed the picture to Nick.

'Good, isn't it?'

'Yes,' said Nick.

'Reckon it means I won't have to go to prison.'

He wasn't going to say anything slushy to his big brother. Nick didn't do slushy.

The two boys were silent for a few moments. Stefan couldn't guess what Nick was thinking. He was just staring at a train picture on the wall. But seeing Mor's picture had given Stefan an idea.

'Nick, do you think Mor would do another picture?'

'What, strings again?'

'No, not strings. A picture of Mrs Tie-String's trainers on a poster. We could write the words LOST. HAVE YOU SEEN THEM? on it. Then we get them photo-something, whatever it is, at the library. Then we put the posters up in different places.'

'You don't want to give up, do you? You mean to find those trainers,' said Nick.

'Yes, Nick, I do.'

'OK. But you will have to ask, not me.'

'Right, I will then.'

Stefan stood up and walked to his bedroom door and opened it. Nick followed him. Stefan led the way down the stairs, practising in his mind what he would say to Mor. There were three things: One, say sorry. Two, would she do a drawing for a poster. And three, could he have a drink. He must get it right.

At the bottom of the stairs, he walked the few steps to the lounge and opened the door. Mor was sitting on the settee reading a book. She looked up as he came through the door, followed by Nick a few steps behind. Stefan took a good deep breath.

'Sorry about the poster, er, no, about the drink, well, what I mean is, well, sorry about the picture.'

The words didn't come out the way he planned. He felt a bit silly standing there. Then as he looked at her, he noticed a tiny smile begin to crinkle her mouth. He watched as it grew into a grin. He found himself doing the same. Then Mor put her arms out. He ran across the room into them. The arms wrapped around his body and for a moment neither spoke. Then suddenly he felt silly again. He was a big boy, and big boys didn't do cuddles. He moved back a little, wondering how Nick was taking it all. Nick wasn't looking at them. He had moved to the corner of the room and was crouching down on the floor looking at something.

'That spider has a leg missing. There should be eight. I've just counted them,' said Nick standing up.

Stefan and Mor got up and moved to where Nick was. Sure enough, in the corner being very still was a spider. They counted the legs aloud together. There were only seven. They counted again. Definitely seven.

'Can they live with one leg gone?' asked Stefan.

'Perhaps they grow a new one, but I'm not sure,' replied Mor.

Then they began to laugh, not at the spider but at themselves. There they were, three human beings staring at a spider on the floor. The spider now had enough of being stared at and had decided to move. It was getting along quite well with one missing leg.

Everyone now felt so much better. They left the spider to its wanderings and sat down on the settee.

'Right, Stefan, get yourself a drink. You said something about a poster, so you can tell me after you've had your drink.'

'Thanks, Mor.'

Stefan got up from the settee and went into the kitchen.
A few moments later he came back with a drink of orange
juice. He sat down on the settee again on one side of Mor.
Nick was on the other side. Stefan downed his drink in
one go. He hadn't realised just how thirsty he was. The
others waited until he had finished. He put his glass down
on the coffee table.

'You needed that,' laughed Mor. 'So tell me about this
poster then.'

'It's an idea I've got about Mrs Tie-String's trainers.
It's about making a 'lost' poster. Mor, would you draw a
picture of Mrs Tie-String's trainers on it, and me and Nick
could write the words LOST. HAVE YOU SEEN THEM?
Then we can get it photo ... what's it called, at the library.
Then we put the posters up in different places.'

'Photocopied is what you mean,' said Mor.

'Yes, and then we can put the posters up in the village.'

'It's a good idea, Stefan, and I know it means a lot to
you to find those dratted trainers,' said Mor, 'but you must
ask Mrs Tie-String first. If she says yes, then I will do the
drawing for you. Is Toby going to help you?'

Stefan didn't know what to say for a minute or two. He
had felt let down by Toby. He wasn't sure if they were still
friends.

'Well, now that Nick's home he can help me,' he said.

Stefan felt his face go red. He saw Mor's smile go away
for a minute.

'I see,' she replied slowly, 'but be careful what you do
and say.'

Stefan wasn't sure what that meant, so he just nodded
his head.

'Anyway, you'd better ring Mrs Tie-String and tell her about your idea. Then leave it for the rest of the afternoon and do something different—a jigsaw maybe or play with your dinosaurs.'

He nearly said, 'But I'm alright now' but thought better of it. Best to do what Mor said, not risk being cheeky. So he said, 'Yes, Mor' instead.

He then picked his glass up and took it into the kitchen. He washed it up and put it away in the glasses' cupboard. He then went into the hall and picked the phone up. A few minutes later he went back to the lounge where Mor was now reading again. Nick wasn't there. Mor looked up as he came towards her.

'Nick has gone to his bedroom to find out about spiders' legs in his big insect book,' she said. 'So, my young detective, what did Mrs Tie-String say?'

'I told her about the poster idea. She said "capital" and then put the phone down. Does that mean yes?' asked Stefan.

'Yes, it does, short and sweet. I expect she wanted to get back to the chickens, and I want to get back to my book now.'

Stefan took that to mean he had to go, so he did. He went upstairs to his bedroom and got out his favourite jigsaw, with a picture of a Tyrannosaurus Rex on it, out of his toy cupboard. He then spent a good hour putting it together. It certainly looked good when he had finished it. He then got his toy dinosaurs out and made up a game where the jigsaw Tyrannosaurus Rex ruled the world and the other dinosaurs had to fetch things for it. Lots of objects in his bedroom became the property of the T-Rex, including three marbles, two felt-tip pens and a dog ornament.

The time went very quickly. Teatime came and went, as well as the evening playing board games with Malc. Nick spent the time learning all he could about different spiders in the world and told everyone not to go near a black lace-weaver spider as it can give a nasty bite! Everyone promised they wouldn't.

Then it was bedtime, so Stefan went to bed. He lay there with his eyes open for a while. Mor had promised she would do a drawing of Mrs Tie-String's trainers. Things were looking up. He could go to sleep now he had a brand new plan.

...

The next morning, Stefan woke up feeling happy again. It was going to be a good day. He jumped out of bed, got washed and dressed and went downstairs to the kitchen for breakfast. Malc had gone to work, but Nick was there. Nick had finished his porridge and was happily eating a piece of toast and jam. Stefan took the bowlful of porridge doled out for him by Mor and sat down at the table.

'Now eat that; it's hot creamy fuel for young detectives,' Mor said.

Mor was always telling him that eating porridge did all sorts of wonderful things to his body. He grinned and took a tiny mouthful as it was sometimes too hot. It was, so he poured some milk on top of it. He took another mouthful. It was still hot but not enough to burn his tongue. He then ate the lot. Afterward he helped himself to toast and marmalade and drank the tea Mor gave him. He set his mug into his empty bowl and put them both on his plate to take to the sink where Mor had started to do the washing up.

Nick had already taken his breakfast things to the sink. He was now picking toast crumbs off the table and eating them one by one. Stefan returned to the sink to start the drying up. He knew that Nick would follow behind him. It was a morning job they both had to help with during the school holidays.

'Right you are, my bonny lads, two clean tea towels,' said their Mor.

Stefan pulled a face. He didn't like being called a bonny lad. It was an unfortunate habit of Mor's. Nick never seemed to notice. They both took a tea towel each and began to dry the breakfast things.

'After you two have finished, I'll show you my drawing, and then the rest is up to you both.'

Stefan said 'Thanks', and Nick began to count the spoons as he dried them, something he did every time they dried the dishes.

It was a normal start to the day.

Just then Stefan heard the sound of the post being pushed through the letter box in the door in the hall. He went to pick it up. There were three letters lying there. He looked at the names on them. The first two were for Malc; that wasn't surprising. Mor said they were usually bills. The third one had his name on it, written in large capital letters.

Stefan was surprised. He didn't often get letters. He took them all into the kitchen and put Malc's down on the now-cleared kitchen table. Then he opened his own letter. There was just one folded piece of paper in it. He unfolded it and began to read.

'WHAT!!' he yelled.

'Everything alright?' asked Mor.

'Yes, no, look at this. It's about the trainers. Look at what it says.'

Mor and Nick both looked over Stefan's shoulder. Nick read the words out loud. 'THE TRAINERS ARE IN THE PHONE BOX.'

Each letter in the words had been cut out of a newspaper.

Stefan didn't wait for Nick or Mor to answer. Talking would waste time.

'I have to go, right now.'

He darted into the hall, grabbed his coat and shoes, put them on and was out of the door before anyone could stop him.

Stefan knew the phone box was a place where anyone could leave anything they didn't want for anyone who would like it. People left old books there and sometimes vegetables. There was an honesty box where people could put a donation that went to charity. Suppose a stranger found the trainers and took them for themselves. He had to get there quickly—run as fast as he could.

The street was very quiet as he ran, and it was raining hard. He began to feel frightened. Suppose it was a trick to get him there. Suppose someone was out to get him. Suppose they had a knife.

There was a car coming, and it was getting nearer. He began to run even faster. The rain was blurring his eyes.

He rubbed them with his wet coat sleeve. It didn't make much of a difference.

He could hear the car close to him now. It stopped. Stefan could run no more. He fell to the ground and prayed as he had never prayed before.

A voice called out.

'Stefan, it's me. Get in the car.'

He recognized the voice immediately. It was Miss Sit-up-straight. What a relief.

He stood up straight away.

'I've found the trainers, Stefan. Get in quick. You're soaking wet.'

Miss Sit-up-straight opened the car door, and Stefan got in.

'Right, I need to get you home quickly so you can get yourself dry,' said Miss Sit-up-straight, starting up the car engine.

Up until then, Stefan hadn't thought about how wet he was, but now he did. He felt cold and he shivered in his seat. He was feeling disappointed too. He had so much wanted to find the trainers himself.

Now Miss Sit-up-straight would take them back to Mrs Tie-String, and that would be that. No hero clapping for him in assembly this time. His head went down. He found himself looking at his feet. He was aware out of the corner of his eye that Miss Sit-up-straight had turned her head briefly to look at him. He tried a quick polite smile, but his mouth couldn't do one.

'Try not to feel too bad about not finding the trainers yourself,' said Miss Sit-up-straight. 'It was just a matter of luck that I found them. I only went to the phone box to see if there were any good books to read, and there they were, the trainers in one corner.'

Stefan tried a smile.

'Look, Stefan, why don't you take the trainers back to Mrs Tie-String after you've got dry and had your dinner. You've done the work asking all of us for our help. You did exactly the right thing. Your parents must be proud of you. And I wouldn't be surprised if Mrs Tie-String hasn't got a reward for you.'

Stefan felt a bit cheered up at hearing this. He hadn't thought about getting a reward. This time his mouth was able to do a polite smile.

'Thank you, Miss Sit-up-straight,' he said.

'You're welcome, Stefan.'

It wasn't long before they were at Stefan's house. Miss Sit-up-straight stopped the car. Stefan said, 'Thank you, Miss Sit-up-straight.'

Miss Sit-up-straight said, 'Mind you get thoroughly dry.' She then handed over the trainers.

Stefan took them and said 'Thank you' again and got out of the car. He closed the car door and watched as Miss Sit-up-straight drove away. He thought it the polite thing to do. He then walked up the front path to his house, opened the door and went in.

'Mor, I'm back,' he called out.

'About time too. You rushed out like a cat with its tail on fire, and I bet you're soaking wet.'

Mor's words bounced down the stairs. It was her I'm-not-at-all-happy voice. He knew he had a bit of explaining to do. Better get it over and done with, then after dinner he could take the trainers round to Mrs Tie-String. Now to just get dry and warm …

···

Getting dry, changing clothes, dinner and explanations were now over. Dinner had been great, explanations not so good. At least Mor had been relieved that Miss Sit-up-straight had brought Stefan home and the trainers had been found. When he said he would like to take the trainers round to Mrs Tie-String's that afternoon, Mor agreed as long as he walked slowly. No more running today, she said. Detecting is one thing, but getting soaking wet was often followed by colds and even flu. Fussing again, he thought, but he agreed.

It was now half-past one. The trainers were in the hall where he had left them. The coat he had worn that morning was still wet. He looked and found his old one, which was a bit small for him as he had grown recently. He put it on. The sleeves didn't come all the way down his arms, but why worry. It was only for the afternoon anyway. He bent down and found some dry shoes and put them on too. Gloves came next, and he was ready.

What he needed now was a bag he could put the trainers in. He couldn't carry them in his hand, even though it had stopped raining. There were lots of bags in the cupboard under the stairs. He went and fetched one. He picked up the trainers to put them into the bag. As he did so, he caught his foot on the side of the hall table, which was next to where all the family coats were hanging. He lost his balance and fell onto his side, tipping the trainers up as he fell.

Something fell out of one of them and rolled a little way from where he was lying. He reached over and picked it up. He gasped with surprise. He recognized the object straight away.

Then in an instant, he knew who had taken the trainers. It all fitted. It could only be one person. It was a huge shock.

For a moment, he lay still on the carpet thinking. What was he to do? There was only one thing he could do. He would have to go and ask the one question which was puzzling him. It was the question 'Why?'

Very slowly, Stefan got up off the floor. He put the object inside the trainers and then put them inside the bag, making sure that the object was where it had been. He opened the front door, took a step outside, then turned and closed the door. The rain had stopped, but the sky was still thick with grey clouds.

He set out on his walk. As he walked, his mind was busy going over all the conversations he had had with The-Front-of-Beyond IBs. How brave he had been to keep going when he was getting nowhere. Then the time when he had come up with the idea of the posters. That hadn't happened.

Then getting the letter and risking his life to go the phone box. He had been brave to face any danger there might have been. He was going to be the hero again. Then it had been Miss Sit-up-straight who had found the trainers and given them to him. So maybe there would be a reward, but it wasn't nearly as good as being a hero.

Detecting was nothing like it was in books and on the telly. He had no idea who had written the letter either. That was a rotten shame.

He had arrived at the house now. He knocked on the door. He could hear footsteps in the hall. He took a deep breath and waited for the door to be opened.

Eventually it did, just a little bit, so that Stefan could see inside. It was wide enough for him to see the person who was standing there. It was his best friend Toby.

Chapter six

'Hello,' said Stefan. Toby opened the door wider to let Stefan in, who took one step inside. Toby closed the door. Stefan said nothing. He took the object out of his pocket and handed it to Toby. Stefan watched as Toby stared at the object, then put it in his pocket.

'Did you know it was gone? I mean, it's your best marble, isn't it—the one that looks like Mars,' said Stefan. Toby nodded.

'Where did yer find it?' he asked.

'In these.'

Stefan took the trainers out of the bag and told Toby all about how the marble had fallen out of them. He also told him about what had happened that morning. He then put the trainers back into the bag.

'It was you, wasn't it, Toby?'

Stefan waited for Toby to say something. Toby didn't say a word, but his face had gone very pale. Very slowly, he nodded his head and looked down at his feet.

'The marble must have dropped out of your pocket when you were bending down,' continued Stefan. 'What I don't know is why.'

Toby lifted his face up. Stefan watched as a single tear trickled down his friend's face. He wiped it away roughly with his sleeve. When he spoke, his voice was high and nervous.

'I went to the post office to post a parcel for my Ma. I was late, and Mrs Tie-String was just about to close for dinner, but she let me in.' Toby stopped speaking and wiped another tear away with his sleeve. He looked down at the floor again and continued speaking.

'After she'd done the parcel, she asked me if I would like to see the chickens. The trainers were by the back door. She must've just taken them off. She was wearing her wellies. I followed her through the back of the shop. She said something about how big they were gettin', the chickens that is. Then she saw that one of them was gone, and she went to find it. It was then I grabbed the trainers and put 'em in my school bag.'

'Why?' repeated Stefan.

' 'Cos she's famous. I want to be famous, but then I got scared in case Ma found 'em under my bed where they were. So I put 'em in the phone box. I did a letter to tell you, but I didn't write my name on it. I thort yer would get me to come with you 'cos I 'elped you in the park. Then we could both say we found 'em and I could be a hero like you. I didn't know I'd lost the marble till yer come.'

Stefan didn't say anything. He was really stuck for words. He had no idea that Toby had wanted to be a hero. For a moment, he felt a bit sad for Toby. Suddenly he remembered the park and the trainer they had found there.

'And there's another thing. The old trainer in the park, did you pinch that too?'

Toby looked up and shrugged his shoulders. 'It was a cow-in-sin-dunce, that's all.'

'And then you ran off and you said it was because of early dinner and your Ma said you had to go home. What was that about then?' continued Stefan.

'She 'ad to go see Doctur Be-well, 'cos she has diabeetus with eating the wrong things. She's there now 'cos she 'as to lose weight and it's a slimming class.'

By now Stefan had 1000 heartbeats hammering in his head. He didn't know what to say. He had learned some things about his young friend he didn't know before, and they were sad things too.

' 'Spose yer not going to be my friend now,' said Toby. 'Anyway, you can go if you want as I need a pee. Close the door after you.'

Toby ran upstairs to the toilet. Stefan turned towards the door. It would be so easy to go now. Easy to leave Toby and take the trainers back to Mrs Tie-String on his own. He would have to tell her that Miss Sit-up-straight had found them in the phone box. But at least he would be the one who had brought them back.

If there was a reward, it would all be his. Toby didn't deserve a reward. After all, friends stick by you and help you. They don't leave you on your own. Right, that was it. Toby had cheated on him.

He was off, no messing. He turned the door handle, opened the door and tiptoed outside. He closed the door quietly after him.

Then he set off in the direction of the post office. His steps were quick at first, but then he began to slow down. He just didn't feel right. He was leaving Toby on his own.

Where had he heard those words recently? He thought for a while. Then he remembered. It was the Reverend Hard-pew, and he was giving a talk in assembly ...

'It's getting near to Easter, everyone. After half-term, you will be learning about how things were getting difficult for Jesus. Lots of people didn't like him and began to plot to kill him. Later on, he was arrested and his friends left him on his own.'

Stefan had thought then about how awful it must be not to have a friend. He thought about Toby. Stefan knew he had no other friends but him. But taking the trainers had been thieving. Thieving was wrong. Toby had been wrong to take them. No, he didn't deserve a friend. Stefan began to walk a bit faster. Then faster still, but the bad feeling wouldn't go away. He stopped suddenly. An old man walking behind him bumped into him. Stefan turned around and said sorry.

'Alright then, but tha looks a bit dowie,' said the man.

Yes, that was just how he felt, dowie. It was a word Mamo used a lot when talking about how her bones ached at the end of the day He had guessed it meant sad because that was just how Mamo looked when she said it.

Stefan nodded his head as he couldn't think of anything to say.

'Then ye need to do something aboot it,' the man called out as he walked away.

Without another thought, Stefan turned around and began to walk back to his friend's house. Why he was doing so, he just didn't know. Neither did he know what he was going to say to Toby.

Chapter seven

When he arrived back at Toby's house, he didn't knock on the door but opened it quietly and went inside. Toby was sitting on the stairs. He looked up in surprise.

' 'Spect you've come back to thump me in the belly?' he said.

'No, shan't do that,' replied Stefan.

'Why? Wouldn't blame you if you did,' said Toby, looking down at his feet.

'Because I, well, I don't know why, but ...' continued Stefan. He stopped talking then. He had run out of words. He could hear a clock ticking somewhere in the hall. It began to hypnotise him with its rhythm.

Tick-tock, tick-tock, tick-tock, tick-tock ...

The ticks formed themselves into words, 'not on my own, not on my own' over and over again. They got louder and shouted in his head until he could bear it no longer.

'Right, we take the trainers back to Mrs Tie-String. Together, I mean,' Stefan suddenly blurted out. He jumped at his own words. Where had they come from?

'How do yer mean? I thort you won't want to be mates now,' said Toby, looking up.

'Well, like, I've been remembering stuff and just—well, I sometimes get stuff wrong, and like your Ma's got that diabeetus and that's not nice, so all that stuff about the marble and the trainers, shall we forget it then?' Stefan swallowed. The words had made his mouth go dry and lumpy. 'Malc says when you want to forget bad stuff, you shake hands.'

Stefan saw a look of surprise come on Toby's face.

'Do yer mean it?' asked Toby.

'Yes,' said Stefan, holding out his hand.

Toby wiped his nose on his sleeve and shoved his hand out.

Stefan took hold of Toby's hand, and together they shook hands.

Toby sniffed a big sniff and said, 'Thanks.'

'Better get your coat and shoes on,' said Stefan. The tight feeling in his mouth had gone, and his words had come back. It was a relief.

'Right, well, sorry about all of the bad stuff. You can have my best marble if yer want. The red Mars one.'

Stefan gave a little smile. It was a kind thought of Toby's. It was the best thing that had happened to him that day.

'Thanks, but no. It's yours, you keep it. But we need to go.'

Stefan waited as Toby grabbed his shoes and coat, which were in the hall, and put them on. Toby opened the front door, and together they went outside. Toby then shut the door.

It was now time to take the trainers back to Mrs Tie-String. Stefan just hoped she wouldn't ask him how he found them. He didn't want to get Toby into trouble, not now that he had decided to be friends. But he didn't want to tell lies either. He wasn't looking forward to going there at all.

...

Stefan and Toby arrived at the post office a quarter of an hour later. Neither of them had said anything to each other. Stefan wondered if it would take time for them to be really relaxed again in each other's company.

The post office was empty of customers as they walked in. Mrs Tie-String was busy stocking up the shelves with envelopes of different shapes and sizes. She looked up when she saw them.

'Hello, boys,' she said.

'Hello, Mrs Tie-String,' said Stefan and Toby together.

'Well?'

Stefan took this as his turn to speak.

'Mrs Tie-String, we have got good news. We have found your trainers,' he said in his best, politest voice ever.

He took the trainers out of the bag and handed them to Mrs Tie-String. She took them from him and hugged them to her chest.

'This is absolutely brilliant. Well done. Very well done. You must have some lemonade. Come through to the kitchen.'

Mrs Tie-String led the way. Stefan and Toby followed behind.

'Sit down there at the table and I will get your a drink. I make it myself, you know.'

Both lads did as they were told. Mrs Tie-String went to the cupboard, got two glasses out and put them on the table. She then went to the fridge, opened the door and took out a large jug of lemonade. She then filled both glasses almost to the top and handed one to Stefan and one to Toby.

'There you are, lads. Drink up, and of course you must both have a reward.'

She then went out of the kitchen and left them alone. Stefan felt a sudden relief come over him. Mrs Tie-String hadn't asked him how he had found the trainers, and they were going to get a reward. He grinned at Toby. Toby grinned back.

Mrs Tie-String came back a few minutes later. In her hand she was carrying two parcels. She sat down at the table.

'I collected these this morning. They were there in my morning delivery. Ordered them for myself, but I reckon you deserve them most. We've got to have progress, you know, pass on the knowledge.'

Mrs Tie-String then handed one to Stefan and one to Toby.

'Well, don't just sit there. Open them,' she said.

Both boys silently did as they were told. The reward was certainly nothing they could have ever expected. They both stared at the gift in front of them.

It was Stefan who remembered his manners first.

'Thank you, Mrs Tie-String,' he said.

'Yep, thanks. I mean, thank you, Mrs Tie-String,' mumbled Toby.

'Well, off you go then, and good work, lads.'

They both took the hint.

Outside the shop, Stefan looked at Toby and Toby looked at Stefan. Stefan saw a slight smile grow on Toby's mouth. It then became wider. Stefan was now unable to contain himself any longer. His lips too began to widen. Suddenly they were laughing. They laughed so much it gave them bellyache. The presents they had been given were a book each about chickens!

'What's yours called then?' Stefan asked Toby.

'*Chicken Runs*,' replied Toby. 'And yers?'

'*The Art of Raising the Perfect Chicken*,'replied Stefan.

'Narsty pecking things, chickens,' said Toby.

'Ugly heads,' said Stefan.

As they began to walk home, they passed Miss Sit-up-straight in the street. They both stopped to let her pass.

'Everything all right then, boys?' she asked.

'Yes, thank you,' they both said together.

'So, Mrs Tie-String has got her trainers back. And I guess you both got a reward,' the head teacher said.

'Yes, we did,' said Stefan, trying to keep his face straight.

Toby suddenly coughed. Only Stefan knew why!

The End

Stefan gets another chance

Chapter one

The whole school was deathly quiet. Miss Sit-up-straight was standing facing them all. Stefan could see she wasn't smiling. Something must be wrong. Nothing serious had happened since Mrs Tie-String's trainers had gone missing. Everyone in The-Front-of-Beyond had heard all about how Stefan and Toby had found them.

Miss Sit-up-straight had summoned them all to a special assembly. It was early afternoon. A special assembly was for only important occasions. Stefan wondered what it was all about. Someone behind him coughed. The sound made him jump. Someone else near the front moved their chair. The squeaking noise reminded Stefan of a mouse he once saw being caught by an owl. Its death squeal had given him nightmares for a week.

The whole school was now waiting for Miss Sit-up-straight to speak. She began to speak, her voice shaky and high.

'Now listen carefully, everyone. I have called this special assembly to tell you that something serious has happened. The Reverend Hard-pew has had an accident. He was in the churchyard this morning about nine-thirty, searching for a gravestone he needed to find. At the same time, Doctor Be-well was on the golf course about to take a final shot in her game of golf. The shot went further than Doctor Be-well intended and hit the Reverend Hard-pew on the side of his forehead. The Reverend Hard-pew fell to the ground.'

Miss Sit-up-straight stopped talking then to drink some water, which she poured into a glass from a jug on a table near to her.

Stefan thought about the golf course. Some Beyonders had said it should never have been allowed to be so close to the church. What if a golf ball broke a window, they said?

It was the first time he had heard about anyone being hit by a golf ball. It must have been some shot. What if the worse had happened and the Reverend Hard-pew was dead? Was that what Miss Sit-up-straight was going to say next? He waited for her to carry on talking.

Miss Sit-up-straight put her glass down on the table and began to speak again.

'It was Mr Fersen the window cleaner who heard the cry and found him. He called an ambulance. It came quite soon, thank goodness, and the Reverend Hard-pew was taken straight to hospital. That's all I know. And now we will say the special Beyonder prayer for the Reverend Hard-pew.'

Stefan along with all the other children in the school knew the special Beyonder prayer. It was one of the first things they learned when they started school.

After saying the prayer, they were told to go back to their classes. Everyone was quiet. The sort of quiet you had at funerals. The rest of the afternoon went by slowly. The bell for home time came eventually. Everyone went home either with their mothers or on their own. No one talked.

All the people in The-Front-of-Beyond had heard the news. Even at home during dinner, everyone was quiet. The evening dragged. Stefan was glad to go to bed. As he lay there, he said the Beyonder prayer to himself. A feeling of sadness hung in the air as his eyes closed in sleep.

It was the same going to school the following day. Even in the playground, no one played much. There were lots of whisperings. Stefan heard some of them. What if the Reverend Hard-pew had died in the night? someone whispered to him. Would that make Doctor Be-well a murderer? Would she go to prison? Stefan shivered at the thought that he might not see her again.

There were some more whisperings in the school hall before assembly and in his classroom later on. Then everyone in his class went quiet for registration. After registration was over, Mrs Wade, Stefan's teacher, stood up to speak.

'Now then, everyone, you all want to know the news about the Reverend Hard-pew. Well it's not as bad as first thought. The Reverend Hard-pew had mild concussion. He is alright now. Doctor Be-well has been to see him. She said he was in good spirits and should be home soon.'

Someone at the back of the class said, 'Hurrah.' Mrs Wade smiled.

'Now you all know,' she continued, 'there are only a few more weeks of term left.'

Stefan along with everyone else said, 'Yes, Mrs Wade.

Mrs Wade continued. 'And Easter is a special time in The-Front-of-Beyond because ... well, you tell me.'

Stefan put his hand up along with lots of others in his class.

'Well, come on, those of you who know the answer, shout it out.'

Stefan along with most of the children in the class shouted, 'The vicar organizes the Easter Fayre.'

Stefan had learned about the tradition of The-Front-of-Beyond Easter Sunday from Mor when he was very little. Every year for as long as anyone could remember, it was the job of the vicar of the church to put on an Easter Fayre in the afternoon of Easter Sunday. The vicar had to invent all the games that were played and hand out all the prizes to the winners.

Everyone looked forward to it. The church was decorated the day before with spring wildflowers which the children picked from the fields. Everyone made or gave something, which was then displayed on window sills or on tables especially put up. It would be really sad if it had to be cancelled.

Stefan waited to see if his teacher would say that was what was going to happen.

'Now, children, just in case you are wondering if The Easter Fayre is going to happen—the answer is yes.'

Stefan breathed sigh of relief.

Some children punched the air.

'Now, everyone, this is important, so listen up. The Reverend Hard-pew wants someone else to organize the games. So all the teachers had a think about who to have ...'

Here Mrs Wade stopped talking and looked around the class. Stefan wondered who it could be. Then she grinned and said,

'All of you. There will be a competition for the two top classes in the school. The idea is to think of some ideas for games we can all join in. Mr Right-page will then judge them and announce the winners in assembly.'

Stefan along with everyone else in the class cheered. How exciting. Stefan was relieved as it was also Mamo's birthday on the same day as the Easter Fayre. She looked forward to it so much.

Maybe he could ask Mamo for some ideas.

His teacher was now raising her hands.

'Now we need to calm down. I know you are all buzzing with excitement, but number work and writing activities come first. Have a think about the competition this evening at home. Write your ideas down and bring them to school tomorrow. Right, I need a volunteer to give out the number books.'

Stefan didn't put his hand up; he was still thinking about Mamo and her birthday. He watched as Shelagh Binnie was chosen to give the books out. When he got his own, he opened it and turned to a clean page.

Oh well, he thought, there was no getting away from it. Ordinary school work had to come first ...

...

When Stefan got home from school, he was in luck. Mamo was there. The lounge door was open, and she was sitting in her favourite chair. He took his coat off, hung it up and then took his shoes off. He found his slippers and put them on. He then went into the kitchen. Mor was making pastry.

He said, 'Hello Mor.'

She looked up and gave him a 'welcome home' smile. Then she said, 'Mamo is here for dinner. Make her a cup of tea, will you, and take it in with your own drink, and do me a favour—talk to her. I've got a pie to make.'

Stefan said, 'Shall I give her a biscuit as well?'

Mor laughed. They both knew Mamo loved biscuits as much as cake.

Stefan took that to mean yes. He filled the kettle from the tap and switched it on. While the kettle was boiling, he helped himself to some squash. He took out a packet of open biscuits from the cupboard and put some on a plate.

The kettle boiled. He then made the tea. He picked up his own drink and the biscuits and took them into the lounge. Nick was there sitting at the table doing his homework. Stefan put his own drink and the biscuits down on the coffee table and went back for Mamo's drink.

He returned carrying it and placed it on the table. She was sitting with her eyes closed. Stefan wondered if she was asleep. He didn't like to wake her up. There was only one way to know if she was really asleep and that was to pick a biscuit up and eat it. It was amazing how the crunching noise of a biscuit being eaten always woke her up. He sat down next to her and took a biscuit. No sooner had he taken a bite out of his biscuit than Mamo was awake and grinning her lots-of-missing-teeth grin.

'Mamo, I've made you a cup of tea.'

Mamo looked at the tea, then at the biscuits. She took one and began to eat it. Stefan waited to speak until she had finished eating it. But she took another one. Again Stefan waited until she had finished, but she took another one while she was still eating the second one. Stefan decided enough was enough.

'Mamo, your tea is getting cold. You don't like cold tea.'

He passed the cup and saucer to her. She took it.

'Thank ye, lad, and after I've drunk it, I'll have a biscuit!'

Stefan took his chance. He got up and took the plate of biscuits into the kitchen just at the right moment when Mamo was drinking her last mouthful of tea. Then he came back and sat down.

'Good cup of tea lad, no biscuits. That's good. Don't tell Mor, but she keeps on giving me them, and too sweet they are, rot your teeth!'

Stefan nodded. Best thing to do, he decided.

'Mamo, can I ask you something?' he said.

'Aye, lad, ask away.'

Stefan gave a shortened version of all that had happened to the Reverend Hard-pew. Then he finished by talking about the competition and how everyone in his class had to think up some ideas.

'Well, Stefan laddie, let us have a think.'

Mamo closed her eyes. Stefan waited for her to speak. Suddenly she laughed.

'Ah dinnae ken about today, but Piggy Racing was the best then. Aye, you had to mak a mask for yursen with a pig face. And you tied it rund your head. Then you got doon on your knees with other kids. Then you had to run making grunts to the end line with the vicar chasing you with a bucket of mud in his hands. The one who won got the mud poured over 'im. You didna know if you were in front 'cos you couldna see. No one ran fast 'cos you dinna want to win. Us all got jumbled up. And then us all got mud spilled on us by the vicar.'

Mamo started to laugh. Stefan loved to listen to Mamo. Her Scottish accent was like listening to music.

Stefan was about to ask if she could remember any more games when Mor put her head around the door to say it was dinner time.

Everything in Stefan's house stopped for dinner. He would have to wait until later to ask Mamo if she knew any more games. Piggy Racing sounded good. He didn't even mind having mud poured all over him. But now his rumbling tummy needed to be filled ...

Stefan lay in bed feeling very pleased that he had lots of ideas for the Easter Fayre. Mamo had remembered some more after dinner. He wondered if Mamo had remembered them because they were all to do with food. He had written them down on a piece of paper.

He got out of bed to check the list which was in his school bag. He found it, brought it back to bed and read the list to himself.

The Balloon Game. Guess the number of balloons in a potato sack. The guess nearest to the right answer wins a prize. Then the bag is emptied and the race is on to catch as many balloons as you can.

The Orange Game. Balance a pencil on top of a floating orange for twenty seconds. Winners get a free orange.

The Cabbage Game. Roll a cabbage down a hill. The person whose cabbage goes the furthest gets another cabbage, which he then has to stand on. The prize is a cabbage to take home.

Stefan felt happy with his list, and along with the Piggy Racing he had a good list of ideas. He put the list back into his school bag, ready for the next day. He then got back into bed and closed his eyes. The next thing he knew, he was dreaming. In his dream, he was being chased by a cabbage, which then changed into a bright red balloon and floated away. Then his dream changed. He was at school and it was assembly and everyone was clapping him. He woke with the clapping still in his ears.

Chapter two

'**N**ow then, class, did anyone manage to think of any ideas for the Easter Fayre?' said Mrs Wade. 'Yesterday you were all buzzing with excitement about the competition.'

Stefan had thought about nothing else all the way to school. To be honest, he had been thinking about it all the time during assembly too and on his way to his classroom. And now his teacher had asked the question he had been waiting for. His hand shot straight up into the air. Other children were putting their hands up too.

'Oh, good, lots of ideas. I hope you all have written them down in your best handwriting,' said Mrs Wade.

Stefan replied 'Yes, Miss' along with lots of others in his class.

'Good. I want you to come up to the front one at a time. Put your sheet of paper with your ideas into this paper bag. Then sit down. This table first.'

Table by table, the children who had brought their ideas to school filed up and put their own piece of paper into the bag. Stefan was among them.

Once that was done, the day continued with the usual classroom activities.

The rest of the week went by neither slowly nor quickly, just the same as most weeks at school. The weekend

passed by the same. Sunday night eventually moved out
of the way to let Monday in. A new week began—the week
Stefan would hear the names of the winners of the best
ideas for this year's Easter Fayre. He couldn't wait to get
to school.

There was an excited buzz in the school playground
when he got there. Very soon the bell went, and everyone
filed into the school hall. The excited buzz followed them
all in and whizzed down each line. In no time, each class
with their teacher was ready for assembly to begin.

To Stefan's surprise, it was the Reverend Hard-pew and
not Mr Right-page who was sitting at the front of the hall.

Stefan stared hard at the Reverend Hard-pew. He
wasn't sure how someone who had been hit with a golf ball
should look. Maybe there would be a dent in the side of his
head. Stefan leaned forward to see him better, but no, the
Reverend Hard-pew looked as he always looked.

Miss Sit-up-straight was standing next to him. She
raised her hand, a sign for everyone to be quiet.

'Good morning, everyone,' she said.

'Good morning, Miss Sit-up-straight,' replied Stefan in
his best polite voice along with all the other children in
the school.

'Now we will all say good morning to the Reverend
Hard-pew, who is well enough to judge the competition.
We are so pleased, Reverend, that your injuries were
not as bad as they could have been. It is good to see you
looking—um—better.'

Stefan did his best polite voice thing again and said
good morning to the Reverend Hard-pew along with
everyone else.

The Reverend Hard-pew then stood up, said 'Good morning, everyone,' and sat down.

'Now everyone,' said Miss Sit-up-straight. 'I expect you all want to know who has won the Easter Fayre competition so over to the The Reverend Hard-pew.'

Miss Sit-up-straight then sat down next to The Reverend Hard-pew who then stood up. He was holding a piece of paper in his hand. There was an expectant hush in the hall.

'Well, everyone, I know you are all wondering who has won the competition. The idea was for the upper school to come up with ideas for games we can all play at The Easter Fayre. I have read them all and there are lots of good ones. I shall keep ten of them to be used if the winner is ill or anything else happens.'

Stefan glanced along his class row. Everyone was leaning forward to listen. His heart began to beat faster. Was his dream going to come true?

'And the winner of the upper classes children's competition for the best idea for games to play at The-Front-of-Beyond Easter Fayre is ...' the Reverend Hard-pew paused. A few moments went by. You could hear a pin drop.

'It's Ian Gallice.'

Everyone clapped. Stefan did too, as he knew it was the right thing to do. Ian Gallice was in his class. He was a quiet lad who worked hard. Stefan didn't know him well, but he knew he lived in a posh house and had the best bike ever and a dad who worked for the government.

Ian would be the one who would start the games and give the prizes out. It wasn't fair. Everyone would say Ian had saved the day. It was just like being a hero. And this time it wasn't Stefan Bell.

Now if it had been himself who had won, then he could have told Mamo, and she would have clapped and eaten lots of biscuits. He really thought Mamo's ideas were brilliant. It just wasn't fair at all.

The clapping eventually stopped. Ian Gallice had got up from his seat during the clapping to walk to the front. He was now standing opposite the Reverend Hard-pew, who was shaking his hand.

'Well done, Ian. It was amazing how many games you could think of using the humble straw ...'

The Reverend Hard-pew then began to list all the straw games that Ian had come up with, but Stefan had stopped listening. Straws were boring. All you did with them is suck juice through them. What was worse was the Reverend Hard-pew was now giving Ian Gallice a prize. It was a Dinosaur Flying Plane. Stefan had always wanted one. Worse still, everyone was clapping again.

Miss Sit-up-straight then stood up and raised her hand. It was a signal to be quiet.

'Well then, everyone. It has been an exciting start to the day. Congratulations to Ian Gallice. And to those who entered and didn't win, better luck next time. And thank you to Reverend Hard-pew for coming this morning. We are so pleased you were well enough to judge the competition. Now it is time, children, to go to your classes.'

And that was it. The school was dismissed, and everyone went to their own classes. Stefan felt numb. He had never felt so deflated before in his entire life. The disappointment in not winning the competition got to him badly. He did his school work alright, but he wasn't the hero now. Someone else was.

In the days after the competition, Stefan got up as usual, went to school, did his homework and all the things he was asked to do, Only with a big difference. His smile disappeared.

Everyone at home knew why he was unhappy. They all knew about Ian Gallice and how he had won The-Front-of-Beyond Easter Fayre games ideas competition.

News travelled fast in The-Front-of-Beyond. Middle-aged and old Beyonders said how nice it would be to have someone young to run the games, new blood for a change.

Stefan's heart ached when he heard people say it in the street. Suddenly Ian was the hero. He was the one whom everyone said had saved the day.

As each day passed, Stefan became more and more unhappy. No one could cheer him up, though they tried hard enough.

...

A week went by, then two. Easter was early that year, so there were not many weeks left to the end of term. The weather had changed from being wet and mild to windy. It stayed windy for a few days. Then the weather improved. The sun came out. After a few days of sun, it became windy again. Then one day the storm began and the wind became a gale.

Mamo said, 'It was some March bluister, an' ye shouldna castna a cloot, til Mey be oot!'

Stefan was used to this favourite saying of Mamo's. Like most Beyonders, he kept his warmest jumpers at the top of the pile in his wardrobe.

Then the gale got worse. Stefan's home and lots of other homes had their power cut off. Beyonders were told to stay in their houses as it could be dangerous to go out.

Then he was told the school had to close as some slates had come off the roof. This was the worst thing that had ever happened to him. Not only had he not won the competition but he couldn't go out either. Life was now a cold prison of misery and loneliness. Would it ever get better?

By the end of the week, the wind was beginning to calm down a bit. Thankfully, the power came back on again. At least now it was warm inside the house. The school was still closed though. Stefan missed not seeing his friends. He would be fine seeing even Ian Gallice. By Sunday, the gale was just about over. By Tuesday, Beyonders were allowed to come out of their houses again. The relief at seeing a bit of sun cheered everyone up.

The following day, Stefan was eating his breakfast when there was a loud knock on the front door. Nick had just finished eating and was reading his favourite spider book in his bedroom. Mor went to answer it. Stefan could hear her talking to someone. It was a man's voice he didn't recognise. He tried to think who it could be.

After a few minutes, he heard Mor say, 'Thank you for telling me,' then the sound of the door closing. In an instant, he thought about Malc. Had something happened to him? Mor came back into the kitchen. She wasn't smiling.

'Something serious has happened,' she said.

Stefan felt his heart miss a beat.

'Not Malc?'

'Oh no, canny lad, it's not Malc. It's Doctor Be-well. She's gone missing. That was a policeman to ask if I had seen her. Well, of course I haven't, but no one has been allowed to go out until this Tuesday. Her cleaner reported her missing this morning. She wasn't supposed to go out like the rest of us, but her bed hadn't been slept in.'

'She's not been sucked out of a window and blown away, has she?' Stefan asked.

He saw a little smile come on Mor's face.

'I doubt it,' said Mor.

'It can happen on planes.'

'Not very often.'

'But it could happen, or she could have been kidnapped by an alien, or she could have run away from home. Maybe she still feels bad about that golf ball hitting the Reverend Hard-pew.'

'No, I don't think she still feels bad about that. After all, she did go and see him in hospital, and they had a nice chat. And aliens, no, this is Scotland. Too cold for aliens! But this is no time for jokes. Doctor Be-well is missing, and the weather we've been having these last few days ...'

Just then the phone rang on the table in the hall. Mor went to answer it. He could hear her talking to someone but not what she was saying. She came back into the kitchen a few minutes later.

'That was Malc,' she reported. 'The police are organising a search party for Doctor Be-well. They are asking for volunteers to help. The police are searching her

house and then spreading out into the nearby fields. They
want us to meet in an hour's time.'

'Can I come?' asked Stefan.

'No, Stefan, this isn't a place for children.'

'But, Mor, I can get into little holes and things.'

'No, it's not giants this time, Stefan. This is a real
person. I don't want you to see anything—well ...'

'You mean a dead body.'

Mor didn't answer. She stopped looking at him and
began to tidy away the breakfast things on the table.

'Right then, I will take you and Nick to Mamo's. I'll
make some sandwiches for you to take and some for Mamo
too. And some cake and cheese, biscuits and fruit. You
both need to take plenty of games and books. It might be a
long day.'

Stefan knew he was beaten. Mor was talking fast with
a definite voice, and she had her 'This is how it is going
to be' look on her face. He would just have to do as he
was told ... that is, unless ... he thought for a while. There
might be a way.

Chapter three

Stefan found that playing with his dinosaurs at Mamo's house was no different from playing with them at home. At least he was able to spread them out on the lounge carpet. There was more room in Mamo's house than in his own bedroom. Nick had disappeared into Popo's old room to look at his war plane books. Mamo didn't mind them going where they wanted to go.

Mamo liked stories too. When he visited her with Mor, she would often tell him stories while Mor did cleaning jobs in the house. The stories were about strange creatures that lived in deep lochs not far away from The-Front-of-Beyond. One was about a strange woman believed to be a mermaid by those who had seen her. Then there was a story about a big monster that had been seen swimming in a deep loch. Stefan would listen and wonder how Mamo knew about them and if they were really true.

Today was no different. Mamo sat down on the carpet and began to tell more strange stories as Stefan played with the dinosaurs.

'But are they true, Mamo?' he said.

'Well, laddie, that's for ye to decide. But folk do say there's a sprite who lives behind the waterfall and it knaws all about strange going-ons and what folk nearby think and do.'

'The waterfall on the river near to Ken's farm?' asked
Stefan.

'Aye, laddie, it's the one. In the cave it lives, the one
near the top of the water. And ye can ask it for a wish so
long as it isn't for yoursen. If it is for yoursen, the sprite
knows, and you'll get canker in your toes!'

Stefan's eyes widened. An idea was coming into his
head. But it would have to wait. He needed to have
his lunch first. And he needed for Mamo to have her
afternoon nap like she usually did. Otherwise the idea
wouldn't work.

'Mamo, I reckon it's time for dinner. Mor's packed us
some sandwiches, and there's biscuits, lots of them, and
fruit and cheese.'

'Biscuits, you say. Well, laddie, I is feeling a bit 'ungry.
Better get yon brother of yours down here.'

'Yes, Mamo.'

...

Stefan smiled to himself. They had all eaten their
sandwiches in the kitchen. Nick had eaten a fair bit of
cake. Mamo tucked into everything. That included a
generous number of biscuits. Stefan just enjoyed it all,
especially the cheese. Nick had then gone back to his
books. Best of all, Mamo had gone to sleep in the rocking
chair.

'Wonderful,' Stefan whispered to himself.

Now was his chance to put his idea into action. The
idea had come into his head when Mamo told him about
the sprite who lived behind the waterfall. That's what he

would do, find the sprite and ask it where Doctor Be-well was. His plan was to be the one to find her. It was a second chance to be a hero.

It would be light until about four o'clock, plenty of time to find her. And Ken's farm was in the opposite direction to Doctor Be-well's house. So there was no danger of bumping into the search party.

He tidied up his dinosaurs that were still on the lounge carpet and put them into a corner of the room so that Mamo wouldn't trip over them. He then tiptoed to the lounge door, opened it slowly and tiptoed through the gap. He then closed the door carefully, making as little noise as possible.

He stood still for a while and listened. There was no noise coming from anywhere. He then found his coat, shoes, gloves and hat and put them all on. He knew it would be cold outside. Best to keep warm.

He then opened the front door and stepped outside, closing the door behind him. He walked quickly along the path and turned left in the direction of the waterfall. He knew the way well. He passed a few mothers with pushchairs all talking to each other. After that, the street was quiet.

He began to walk a bit quicker. As he walked, a thought came into his head. What if the sprite wouldn't grant him his wish to find Doctor Be-well? What would he do? He really did want to find her. She was a nice doctor. When he had fits as a young kid, she always came and made him better. He was thinking so hard, a sudden voice behind him made him jump.

'Hullo.'

Stefan turned around. It was Jamie.

Everyone in The-Front-of-Beyond knew Jamie. Some kids called him names just because he was different. Mor had said it was wrong to call people names as it was un-rispectful, or was it dis-ripectful? Something like that.

'Whit's yer name?'

'Stefan.'

'Whit yer doin'?'

'Going for a walk.'

'Get the polis.'

Stefan wasn't surprised at Jamie wanting to call the police. It was one of Jamie's sayings. Jamie stood for a while looking at Stefan. Then he turned to walk away.

'See ye efter,' he called out over his shoulder.

'Yes, see you, Jamie.'

Stefan carried on walking. After a while, he could hear footsteps behind him again. He turned around. It was Jamie.

'Whit yer doin'?' Jamie asked again.

'Going for a walk.' Stefan couldn't think of anything else to say.

'Get the polis.'

Stefan just didn't know what to do. He needed to get to the waterfall. Time was going, but he couldn't just ignore Jamie. There was a good chance that Jamie might follow him. Even worse, he could fall into the water. He had seen Jamie fall over in the street once or twice. The only thing to do was to take him home and then run as fast as he could to the waterfall to make up for lost time. Jamie lived a few streets away from where they were.

'Come on. Jamie. Home. See your Ma,' said Stefan.

'Ma, tea,' said Jamie, jumping up and down.

They set off together.

Stefan began to walk a bit faster, but Jamie wasn't in any hurry to go home. He insisted on walking with his head down, looking at things on the pavement. Every now and then, he stopped and picked things up. Sometimes it was a leaf or just a stone. He always put them in his right-hand coat pocket. At first Stefan waited for him, but after a few times of Jamie stopping, Stefan could take no more.

'Come on, Jamie. Ma, tea.'

'Ma, tea,' said Jamie, jumping up and down.

Jamie began to walk a bit quicker, but after a while he began to slow down again and stopped to look at something on the pavement. This time it was a big crack. He bent down to look more closely at it. Then he felt along the crack with his finger. Then he jumped up and down. Then, to Stefan's relief, he carried on walking.

This was fine for about ten minutes. Then Jamie stopped again. This time it was because he saw a cat. Stefan didn't know that Jamie didn't like cats. The minute he saw the large tabby, he turned around and ran as fast as he could go. Stefan ran after him. Eventually he caught up with Jamie.

'It's alright, Jamie. It's gone now.'

Jamie stopped running. At least they were now quite a bit nearer to where Jamie lived.

'Come on, Jamie. See your Ma.'

'Ma, tea,' said Jamie, jumping up and down once more.

Stefan looked at his watch. There wasn't much of the afternoon left, and he hadn't even started to walk to the waterfall. There was so much to do— find the sprite, find out where Doctor Be-well was and then find her. It wasn't going according to plan. But there was nothing he could do. He had to see Jamie safely home.

Then Jamie stopped again. This time it was to look up at the sky.

' 'Elicoptar,' said Jamie excitedly.

Stefan couldn't hear the sound of a helicopter, but he very soon did. Then he saw it. It was moving very quickly.

' 'Elicoptar,' said Jamie again, jumping up and down.

Suddenly, Jamie darted into the road to watch it move across the sky.

It was just at that minute that a car raced down the road. Its bright headlights blazed through the afternoon greyness.

It was coming straight towards Jamie. Stefan dashed into the road and grabbed Jamie's arm, pulling him backwards. There was a screech of brakes, then a flash of metal at one side of Jamie, knocking him down. The car didn't stop but sped away into the distance.

Everything that happened next was in slow motion, as though he was dreaming, but in bits that didn't join up. The first bit was kneeling on the road shouting for help. The next bit was seeing Jamie's mother and then an ambulance which somehow appeared from nowhere. Then Nick was there, and he was lying on the road, or was it Stefan himself lying on the road?

The next thing was his mother's face bending over him and a voice saying, 'Stefan, it's me, it's alright,' then nothing.

...

He woke the next day to the sound of birds singing outside. It was just getting light. Strange that Mor hadn't woken him with her usual 'Time for school now' greeting. Maybe it was Saturday or Sunday and everyone was having a lie-in. Then he heard a child's voice, or was it a cry quite close to him? This didn't make sense. Something was wrong. He tried to sit up, but his head felt strange, so he lay down again. But in that second, he had seen a bit of what was around him.

It wasn't his bedroom at home. Where was he?

He tried turning his head to one side. That was better. To his surprise, in a bed close to his was a boy about his own age, and standing next to his bed was a lady in a nurse's uniform. She was turning the boy over to face the other way.

Immediately he knew where he was. He was in hospital. He must be hurt. Then bits of memory came back to him, then some more. Finally it came, the picture memory of the fast car and Jamie lying on the road.

The sudden memory of the accident frightened him. Now it was his turn to cry. The nurse, having finished helping the other boy, who had cried out in his sleep, came up to him.

'It's alright, Stefan. You are in hospital.'

'I want Mor and Malc ... I want ...' A lump in the throat was making it hard for him to talk.

'You will see them soon, Stefan. Time for a bit more sleep. It will make you feel better. Then when you wake up, you can choose your own breakfast.'

Stefan liked her voice. It calmed him a little.

'Now close your eyes.'

Stefan did so. It was quiet now, and his eyes were beginning to feel heavy. Everything drifted away once more.

He woke up about an hour later, just in time for a wash, which a nurse did, and then breakfast. Two other nurses came to change his bed. He sat in a chair until they had finished. The nurses then went to the next bed. He got back into bed feeling a lot better.

Then another nurse came and stuck something in his ear and did some other hospital things too. She said the doctor would come and see him later on.

'Would you like some books to look at, Stefan?'

'Yes, please.'

The nurse went away and then came back with some books.

'Here you are,' she said, handing them to him.

'Thank you,' he said.

He looked at the books and then chose one to read. He started to read it, but his mind kept wandering off. Every now and then, he looked at the clock. Mor and Malc would be coming to see him. That was nice in a way, but what would he say to them when they came? They would want to know why he had left Mamo's house.

The time went by very slowly. He kept on looking at the clock. It was wooden with all the numbers in different colours. The hands were thick and bright yellow. Next to the clock was a poster with all the letters of the alphabet. He closed his book and stared at the poster. He began to make words up with the letters, ones that had to do with monsters.

He was still doing this when he heard a noise. Suddenly, the swing doors opened and some grownups came through. With them were Mor and Malc. They saw him and waved. He waved back. They were here and were now walking up to him. The time had come.

Chapter four

'Stefan, my mo stoirín, how are you?' said Mor, giving him the biggest hug ever.

He hadn't been called mo stoirín in a long time. Malc had said it meant 'my little darling'. It made him feel a bit silly when she said it, like the sort of thing you said to girls.

'Alright,' he said, giving his best smile.

Malc found two chairs and brought them to the side of his bed.

'How are you doing then?' asked Malc with a big grin.

This was better, more like it. Man to man.

'Fine, Malc.'

'Had your breakfast?'

'Yes, porridge and toast with jam and orange juice.'

'Trust Malc to talk about food. Anyway, I've got you something,' said Mor.

She passed a carrier bag to him. 'Some of your favourite things from home.'

Stefan opened the bag and looked inside. There were quite a few things in it. He recognised his four favourite dinosaurs straight away. He took them out and laid them carefully on the bed.

'Thanks, Mor.'

He then looked inside the bag again. There was a tin which he knew belonged to Nick. He took it out and put it on the bed next to the dinosaurs.

'Nick says he wants the tin back, but you can have what's inside,' said Mor.

He was just about to open it when the doctor walked up to his bed. He had arrived on the ward a few minutes ago to start his rounds. Stefan had noticed him enter when he'd been making up monster words. There was a nurse with the doctor. She drew the curtains around his bed.

'So this is Stefan,' said the doctor. 'Saw you yesterday, but you won't remember me. You had a funny turn.'

'Yes,' said Mor. 'I guess he must have heard the car and run down the road. Jamie does wander sometimes. Goodness knows just what speed that car was doing. And not stopping like that. How anyone could hurt a child and not stop. Well, our Stefan got Jamie's Ma, and he must have run like the wind. But it's ...'

Stefan saw Malc nudge Mor in the arm. It was something he did when Mor was spraffing on a bit.

'Well,' said the doctor, 'it sounds as though you were very brave.'

'Yes, you were very brave. And it was just a little fit, mo stoirín, just ...'

Mor was off again. This time Malc put his hand on her arm. Stefan heard him whisper 'Shush', and she stopped talking.

'Alright, Stefan, let's have a look at you,' said the doctor.

The doctor then did doctor things and said kind words, but Stefan felt horrible. Bad words were whispering in his head.

You're not a hero ...

You left Mamo.

The whispering got louder.

Jamie got hurt.

Your fault.

Then the whispering got louder still.

Your fault.

What made it worse was the doctor saying he was fine and it was just he'd had a shock and he would be able to go home soon. And Mor and Malc smiling at him and everything being nice like the presents in a bag and the nurse being kind and being allowed to choose his own breakfast and the clock with yellow hands. It was all too much.

His head had too much in it. It was going to burst.

'NO,' he shouted, holding his head in his hands.

The ward went silent for a few minutes. Then lots of things happened all at once. The doctor said something to the nurse, and she went away.

Mor sprang out of her chair, rushed to his side and started hugging him. Malc picked up the dinosaurs which had fallen on the floor and arranged them neatly on his locker, his very favourite one in the front. The doctor then said something to Malc which Stefan didn't hear. Then the nurse came back and gave him a drink and a pill to take. Then he began to feel sleepy.

...

When he next opened his eyes, everyone had gone except Mor. She was sitting on a chair near him reading a book. He looked at her. She meant well, even though she went on a bit. He really was glad to see her.

The things that had happened to him that morning came back into his mind. It was just as well, as now was his chance to tell Mor what really happened. It was the right thing to do. He knew it. If it meant going to prison when he was better, then he would face it like a man. That's what Malc would say.

He must have made a little noise, because she looked up.

'Oh, you're awake then. You've been asleep for a couple of hours.'

'Mor, I've got to tell you something.'

'Is it important?'

He was about to say yes when the swing doors opened and in came a lady pushing the dinner trolley.

'Oh, it's dinner time. Tell me later. I'll just nip down to the canteen and have a sandwich. I want to see Jamie too. Then I'll come back. And Malc is bringing Mamo and Nick to see you this afternoon a bit later on, so enjoy that dinner of yours.'

She then walked away.

It was no good. He had to tell Mor on her own, then she could decide whether to tell Malc, Nick and Mamo. His future lay in her hands.

Chapter five

Despite everything, Stefan managed to eat his dinner and his pudding too. It was the sensible thing to do. After all, he might have to live on bread and water in prison.

He was expecting Mor to come back straight away, but she didn't. He lay there for a while, wondering what to do. Then he remembered he'd been given some books to read. He had no idea where they had gone to. Maybe they were in his locker, but was he allowed out of bed? Well, no one had said he wasn't.

He was just about to get out of bed when the swing doors opened, and in came Toby and his Ma. They looked around for a few seconds. Then they saw him and walked up to his bed.

'Now then, Toby, just four minutes,' said Toby's Ma. 'You sit down and I'll meet you by the door. Remember now, just four minutes.'

She then walked away, and Toby sat down. He looked all around him and then at the floor.

Stephen decided to be the first to speak.

'Dinner was good. So was pudding, strawberry mousse.'

'Not chocolate then?' asked Toby.

'No, not chocolate.'

Silence.

'Did yer know they found Doctor Be-well?' said Toby.

'No, where?'

'In a barn, puggled in a corner!' Toby grinned.

'What do you mean?'

'Yer know what puggled means, like when your eyes won't stay open. Someone rung her in the night. Said they was all ill, and she went off in her car to the hoose but they wasn't ill at all. It wasn't them that rung. So she came back, only she dint 'cos she got some of the way and then it was too windy, so she 'ad to stop. So she got out and walked to this barn and went in, then she went to sleep. They found her behind some hay. Lots of peeple had been out looking for her, and they had a helicopter looking too ... Polis said it was all pretend to get Doctor Be-well out of the hoose 'cos when she was away, some thieves went in and pinched some of her jewellery. Then next day, when peeple were looking for her, the thieves came back and pinched some plates. Polis said they were an-teek.'

'What?'

'Yer know—old and valible,' said Toby. 'Then the thieves drove off really fast and Jamie got knocked down, but Mor said he was just concussed, and he's in a room all by himself, and he's comin' home tomarra. I know 'cos Mor told my Ma at the 'airdressers.'

Toby took a big breath. He then turned his head and looked at the clock.

'And I 'av to go now 'cos Ma said four minutes, and time's up by that clock over there. Oh, and school is still closed 'cos lots of slates came off the roof. Fancy stone skimmin' when yer come out?'

Stefan loved stone skimming. He was good at it. Getting just the right stone was the most important thing. It had to be flat. Then you had to throw it sidearm so it bounced on the water. It took a bit of practice to get it right. Maybe if they all gave him a last wish before he went to prison ...

Stefan just nodded his answer to Toby. Best to keep quiet.

'See yer then,' Toby said.

'See you, Toby.'

That was it. Toby stood up and walked away.

Stefan thought about what he had just heard. It had been a really long and fast speech, but he had got the gist of it. Doctor Be-well had been found, and Jamie would get better. What a relief. He wouldn't have to go to prison. He could just go home and everything would be alright again.

Then another thought came into his mind. He didn't have to tell Mor now about leaving Mamo and Jamie following him. No one needed to know. Best of all, he could be a hero again for getting help for Jamie. Chances were Jamie wouldn't remember what had happened anyway. The best thing to do was just keep quiet.

He felt so much better. He put his head back on the pillow and closed his eyes. Maybe the doctor would let him go home soon. He thought about what Toby had said about school being closed. That was a shame in a way as he liked school most of the time, but at least he wouldn't have to face Ian Gallice. He might just start bragging about his straw games ideas. They all sounded silly anyway, alright for little kids.

Mamo's ideas were better. It was her birthday soon. Maybe ... was that her voice? He snapped his eyes open. There she was standing. Was it a vision? He screwed his eyes up tight.

'Hey now, laddie, it's me. Keep thee heid!'

That was Mamo alright. She was no ghost. A ghost didn't talk like she did.

He opened his eyes.

'Mamo, it's you.'

'Am fair puckled, laddie, and I needs to sit doon. Am pure dun in. The rest of them are on the way. Mor got talking and so I kept going. Nick stopped to pick up a ... it was a ... well, it was something on the floor. Malc stopped with him. How ye doing?'

'I'm good, Mamo.'

Just then, the swing door opened and in walked Mor, Malc and Nick. Mor was in front. She arrived first. She bent down and gave him a kiss. He didn't mind the kiss. After all, no one knew him in hospital.

'I met Toby's Ma in the corridor. We had a right guid blether together, and I forgot about the time.'

Stefan smiled. He wondered who had been doing most of the blethering, Toby's Ma or Mor.

Mor stepped to one side. Then Malc came up to his bed, ruffled his hair and went to get another chair. Nick sat down at the end of the bed, then after a few minutes, he slid under it. He emerged with a dead cockroach, which he deposited on the top of Stefan's locker.

'A fine specimen,' Nick said. 'It's got all its legs.'

Stefan accepted this gift with good grace. It reminded him that Nick had put a tin in with the gifts Mor had brought him. He reached down, opened his locker and took the bag out. He found the tin and took it out. He opened it. Inside was a dead beetle. It was cradled in a big tuft of grass. Stefan lifted the cockroach carefully and placed it next to the beetle.

'Thanks, Nick.'

Nick grinned.

Stefan noticed there were some more things in the bag. One of them was in a plastic bag. He looked to see what it was. It was a packet of biscuits. Mamo must have donated them. He took the biscuits out of the bag and laid them on the bed. The packet had been opened. Stefan guessed there were about three missing. He saw Malc wink at him. He winked back.

Just like Mamo. What a great family he had, even Nick who was now arranging all the dinosaurs on top of the locker in order of size.

There was just one thing left in the bag. It was a small pouch. He took it out.

'Mamo wants you to have this,' said Mor.

He opened the pouch. Inside was an object the size of a coin. It was wrapped up in silver tissue paper. He undid the paper. What he saw took his breath away. It was a war medal.

'It belonged to your Popo. It's from the First World War.'

Stefan held the medal in his hand. It was bronze and star-shaped with crossed swords. It had a red, white and blue ribbon attached to it. It looked very important. He didn't know what to say. He looked up at Mor.

'I know what you're thinking. It takes your breath away. Your Popo served in France during the war.

He was a brave man. It's a brave thing to do to save someone's life.'

From the moment Stefan saw the medal, he wanted to own it. It was like finding treasure. He looked down at it again. Keeping it would mean he had to hide the truth about Jamie's accident forever. It was the only way now he could be a hero. It took only a moment to decide what to do. He was going to have the medal. It would belong to him, and no one else was going to have it.

He looked up. Everyone was looking at him. He took a deep breath in and then out. Mor had once said that was what you did when you wanted to feel calmer.

Then he said, 'Can I keep it forever?'

'Yes,' said Mor. 'It belongs to you now. You deserve it.'

Yes, he thought, he had done lots of good things in his life in The-Front-of-Beyond. Didn't those deserve a medal?

Chapter six

It was quiet on the ward now. Mor, Malc and Nick had gone. They had talked a bit about how things were in The-Front-of-Beyond and the damage the wind had done. They had also talked about Doctor Be-well and how glad they all were that she was found safe and sound.

They had taken the medal home for safe keeping. He had been left with a dead beetle, a dead cockroach, a packet of biscuits and a big bunch of grapes. Malc had brought the grapes because, as he said, 'They were full of vitamins.' Stefan didn't usually eat them at home, but because Malc had brought them, he ate quite a few when everyone else had been talking.

He decided to eat a few more now just to pass the time. He had just put the next one in his mouth when the nurse came. She asked him how he felt.

'A lot better,' he said. In a way it was true. His body did feel a lot better, but like before his mind didn't feel quite right.

The nurse then did some hospital things that nurses do.

'Well, Stefan, you certainly are a lot better,' she said. 'If the doctor says it's alright, you might be able to go home tomorrow.'

Stefan grinned. Home. Yes, his mind would be better at home. It was probably being in hospital that was making his mind feel all wrong.

The nurse then went away. He looked around him. What to do next? There were toys in the ward he could play with, and his own dinosaurs. And then there would be sandwiches for tea. Time would pass.

And so it did.

...

The following morning, the doctor came. He asked Stefan some questions. Then the doctor did the same hospital things he had done before.

'Good, everything is back to normal. How does going home suit you?' said the doctor.

'Yes, please,' said Stefan.

Just at that moment, Mor arrived. Sefan told her the good news. She threw her arms around him. It was such a tight hug, he could hardly breathe ...

'At last, oh happy day. It will be a relief to have you at home. Nick is spending a few days at Mamo's house, so it will be nice and quiet for you. But, my mo stoirín, no rushing around. You will have to take it easy for a few days.'

'Yes, Mor,' he managed to sputter, his mouth surrounded by a hairy jumper.

'Yes, that's right, but not for too long. Take care, Stefan,' said the doctor as he walked away.

Mor then let go of him. It was a relief. He could breathe again.

'Right, you'll need some clothes. I'll go and get them,' she said.

And off she went.

Stefan gathered his things up and put them back into the bag that they came in. He then ate the rest of the grapes and half of the packet of biscuits Mamo had given him. He put his dinosaurs in the bag. The top of his locker was cleared now except for the books the nurse had let him read. He had read two of them already. There were four of them altogether. He picked the third one up, just to pass the time while waiting for Mor to come back with his clothes. He began to read. The minutes ticked by ...

'Right, it was a bit of a rush, but I've made it.'

Stefan jumped at the sound of Mor's voice. He had been enjoying the book so much he hadn't heard her come back.

'Here are your clothes,' she said, taking them out of a bag and handing them to him. 'I'll pull the curtains round your bed, then you can get dressed.'

She did so.

Stefan then got out of bed and began to get dressed. It felt strange to be wearing clothes again instead of pyjamas. His whole body felt heavy. He put the pyjamas in the bag with his slippers and put his coat and shoes on. He was ready to go.

Stefan looked out of the window all the way home in the car. Mor was happy for once just to drive and not talk. When they got home, he got out of the car, and Mor carried his case into the house. She then took it upstairs. Stefan opened the lounge door and went in. He looked around it all. It looked the same, only smaller.

'I know what you're thinking,' said Mor, who had just come back. 'It all looks small. That's because you've got used to the bigness of the hospital ward. I remember thinking the same once myself when I had appendicitis and ... whoops, here I go again and you probably tired out.'

He did feel tired, but not in the way Mor may have thought. His body felt alright, but his head still felt wrong.

'I'm dying for a cuppa. Then you can have a lie-down on the settee. Milky tea and a biscuit?'

'Yes, please.'

She went into the kitchen.

Stefan sat down on the settee and waited for his drink. In a few minutes, Mor returned with the drinks on a tray and a biscuit each on a plate. His mug of tea was just as he liked it, milky sweet and not too hot. The biscuit was so fresh, it crumbled in his fingers. They sat together in silence for a few minutes until both of them had finished eating and drinking.

'Right then, time for a lay down,' said Mor, fetching a blanket from behind the settee.

Stefan did as he was told. Maybe if he rested enough, in a few days' time he might be well enough to go stone skimming with Toby. A rest might help to clear his head.

Chapter seven

Stefan was now beginning to hate the settee with a vengeance. On day two after coming out of hospital, he had been allowed to play in the morning, but in the afternoon he had to have a lie-down on the settee. On day three, it had been the same. And Mor had definitely said no to stone skimming.

When he woke up on day four, he decided enough was enough. It wasn't just the settee. It was his head. It hadn't got better. The little voice which had got louder in the hospital had come back. It was telling him he had done wrong and that he needed to do something about it. And he knew what he had to do.

'Mor, can we go and see Jamie this afternoon?'

He had just finished eating his breakfast. Better to ask now than risk another boring afternoon on the settee.

Mor was in the middle of swallowing a mouthful of toast. Stefan crossed his fingers behind his back and waited for her to speak. He watched as she poured herself another cup of tea.

'Well,' she said, taking a sip of tea, 'You've rested up these past few days, and it's promising to be a fair day, so yes, why not. I'll give his Ma a ring a bit later on.'

'Thanks, Mor,' Stefan said, uncrossing his fingers.

'But not for long, mind. Why not read a book on the settee this morning instead of playing with your toys? Keep your energy for this afternoon.'

'Oh, but ...'

'No buts, Stefan. Reading this morning, out this afternoon.'

It was no good arguing. The settee had won again. He went upstairs to his bedroom and found two books he liked. While he was fetching them, Mor rang Jamie's house. He heard her on the phone as he walked downstairs. He waited until she had finished speaking.

'Right then, Jamie's Ma is out, but his grandad is there as he is looking after him. He said he was sure Jamie would like to see Stefan and it's fine to come. We agreed on two o'clock.'

'Thanks, Mor.'

Stefan felt relieved that Mor had arranged everything. He walked back to the lounge and the now so very familiar settee. He sat down to read the books he had fetched from his bedroom. Later they had soup and bread together, followed by cake and tea.

So the morning went and the afternoon arrived.

'Right, time to go,' said Mor after doing the washing up. 'It's a fair day, but it's cold, so you need your thick coat, scarf, hat and gloves.' She fetched her coat and shoes from the hall.

'But we'll be in the car,' said Stefan.

'No arguing. After all, you have to walk to the car. I don't want you catching a cold.'

'Yes, Mor.' He went into the hall, found them all and put them on. 'Oh, and I need to fetch something from upstairs.'

Without waiting for an answer, he dashed up the stairs, found what he wanted and came down again.

Mor was waiting for him.

'What was all that about?' she said.

'It's for later,' he replied.

He didn't wait for her to answer but opened the front door and walked to the car. Mor followed him, locking the door behind her. She opened the car doors and they got in. Once or twice during the journey to Jamie's house, she glanced at him in an odd way. Stefan wondered if she was going to ask him any questions. So he began to talk about Mamo's birthday and what to buy her. It worked, and they arrived at Jamie's house without any searching questions.

They both got out of the car. Stefan followed Mor down the path to the front door of Jamie's house. He was now feeling very nervous. His mouth had gone dry, and his heart was beating faster than normal. Mor rang the doorbell. They waited. Eventually it was opened by a man with a round face and glasses. He was wearing jeans, a blue-grey striped jumper and grey trainers. He was smiling. Stefan liked him straight away.

'Hello, I'm Jamie's grandad, and you must be Mrs Bell, and this young man must be Stefan.'

'Yes, and you don't look old enough to be a grandad,' said Mor, laughing.

Stefan thought he did, but then everyone over thirty-five was old to him.

'Come on in,' said Jamie's grandad.

Stefan followed Mor and Jamie's grandad into the hall and then into the lounge. A cosy fire was burning.

'Come and get warm. Fiona, my daughter, Jamie's Ma, is at the hairdresser's, so it's just me and Jamie. Fiona has made some of her black bun, and I know how to make a good cup of tea.'

'Thank you, how lovely.'

Stefan sat down next to Mor on the settee. He was feeling worried now as well as nervous as Jamie wasn't there. Jamie's grandad must have known what Stefan was thinking as he called out from the kitchen.

'Jamie is just in the bathroom cleaning his teeth for the umpteenth time. It's a habit of his. We have tried to stop him from doing it, but then he gets really upset. He'll be down in a minute.'

Sure enough, Stefan heard the sound of the bathroom door opening, then footsteps coming down the stairs. The lounge door opened and in came Jamie. He had a bright smile on his face.

'Whit yer doin'?'

'I'm doing fine,' said Stefan.

It wasn't true, but he had to say something.

'Nice to see you, Jamie, and how are you doing?' asked Mor.

Jamie took hold of Mor's hand and shook it enthusiastically. He was still shaking her hand when his grandad came in with a tray of tea and black bun.

'Jamie, time for tea.'

'Tea,' said Jamie, sitting down on a chair near the fire.

Stefan sat up straight as Jamie's grandad put the tray down on a coffee table in front of them. It looked very posh. He gave them all a plate and a serviette. Jamie put his plate and serviette on the floor.

'Now then, Jamie, best manners.'

Jamie grinned but left his plate and serviette on the floor. No one said anything.

Stefan watched as Jamie's grandad poured out the tea and handed a cup to everyone. He handed out slices of the black bun and then sat down on the chair opposite Jamie.

Stefan saw Mor look admiringly at the black bun.

'What a treat,' she said.

Stefan thought back to when he had first tasted black bun fruit cake. He had been little at the time. Mor had said it was a treat that people ate at Hogmanay. He hadn't known what Hogmanay was then but had soon found out. He had stared in wonder at the cake covered with pastry and bulging with mixed fruits and spices. It looked wonderful. It tasted even more wonderful.

He looked now at the slice of black bun on his plate. Oh, how he wanted to take a bite of it, but a voice in his head was whispering to him. He had something to do first, and it was more important than taking a mouthful of black bun. He took a deep breath and began to speak.

'Mr—er—Jamie's grandad, I have something to say to Jamie, and it's important.'

Stefan looked directly at Jamie. He didn't want to see how the grown-ups would look when he was speaking.

'Oh, OK, Stefan,' said Jamie's grandad, sounding surprised. 'Fire away.'

Stefan took a deep breath and began to speak. He started his story with the day he found out at school he hadn't won the competition for inventing new games for

The-Front-of-Beyond Easter Fayre. He told them about
how much he'd wanted to be a hero and how he'd wanted
to find Doctor Be-well. He told them of the day he'd set out
to find the sprite that lives behind the waterfall.

The room was very quiet as he spoke. The only noise he
could hear was the crackling of the coal on the fire.

He had to swallow a few times as he was speaking
because his mouth had gone very dry. He had no idea if
Jamie was listening or understanding what he was saying,
but he didn't give up. He finished his story at the bit about
the helicopter and how Jamie had run into the road and
the car had come and he had pulled him away.

Then he stopped speaking.

Jamie now had his eyes closed, but Stefan was
determined to go on with his story.

His eyes had gone misty, so he wiped them on his
sleeve. He took another deep breath and began again.

'And so, Jamie, I have come to say sorry and to give you
this.' He swallowed a lump that had come into his throat,
reached into his pocket and took the medal out that Mamo
had given him. He then told Jamie all about the medal.
He got up and walked across to where Jamie was sitting.
Jamie still had his eyes closed, so Stefan placed the medal
gently on the arm of his chair. Then he spoke once more.

'It's for you, Jamie, because you are a friend to
everyone.'

Then he went and sat down.

The room was now so quiet you could hear a pin drop.
Even the fire had given up crackling. For a few moments,
no one spoke. Stefan dared to look to one side at Mor. She
was wiping her eyes too, not on her sleeve but on a dainty

handkerchief with the letter M on it. Then he looked at Jamie's grandad, He was looking at his feet. Then he looked up.

'Stefan, there is another way of showing courage. That is telling the truth, and that is what you have done today.'

He then got up, walked to the chair where Jamie was asleep and picked the medal up. He walked to where Stefan was sitting and put the medal on the settee next to him.

'This really belongs to you, lad. Take it. This medal is part of your family. As for Jamie, he is always wandering around with no sense of danger. Chances are when he saw that helicopter he would have wandered into the road for a better look and that car, well ... what you did that day may have saved his life.'

'But Jamie got hurt and ...'

Stefan could say no more. Tears were now spilling over his eyelashes and down his face. He buried his face in his hands and cried.

He felt Mor's arm circle his shoulders and gently pull him to her side. He smelled her homemade rose petal perfume. He felt her handkerchief dry his eyes.

'It's alright, my mo stoirín. Everything is alright.'

'But ... '

'No buts now. Sit up straight and smile, because I think Jamie is waking up.'

Stefan looked up. Sure enough, Jamie had opened his eyes.

Stefan stood up and walked to where Jamie was sitting. He knelt down by his chair.

'Whit yer doin'?'

'I've come to see you,' said Stefan.

'Yes,' said Jamie's grandad, 'and that tea is stone cold. I'm going to make some more and then we will have ...'

Jamie's grandad lifted the plate of black bun up.

'Black bun,' said Stefan.

Mor and Jamie's grandad laughed together. Jamie jumped out of his chair and did two jumps in the air.

The rest of the afternoon was spent drinking tea and eating black bun. Stefan felt much better, although crying had made him feel tired. His head was lighter though. Gone was the nagging voice. Soon it was time to go home. They said their goodbyes and thank yous for the cake and tea. Mor put the medal in her handbag. Stefan promised he would visit Jamie whenever he could.

In no time at all, Stefan was sitting in the front seat of the car with Mor driving. He looked at her once or twice. She wasn't smiling though, and he wondered if she was a bit cross. Had she just pretended not to be cross in front of Jamie and his grandad? He began to feel a bit nervous again. He plucked up courage and spoke.

'Mor, will I go to prison?'

'Prison! Whatever for?'

'Well, for when I was in hospital and not telling you about what really happened and leaving Mamo on her own.'

Stefan looked at Mor. She didn't answer for a while. It wasn't a good sign. After a while she spoke.

'I'm not going to answer that. Instead, I am going to ask you a question.'

Stefan felt his mouth go dry again. He waited for the question. Would it be a hard one? After a few moments, it came.

'Stefan, do you love your family?'

Of all the questions there were, Stefan didn't expect this. It gave him a shock.

'Yes, Mor,' he answered quickly.

'That's good, as I might have a job for you.'

Silence. Stefan had never known Mor to be so quiet. After a while, she spoke again.

'Stefan, the job might be a bit hard. Will you do it?'

'Yes, Mor,' he answered again.

Silence again. What was this job? Stefan wondered.

By now they had reached home and were pulling into the drive. He reached down and undid his car seat belt. Mor did the same. She turned to him and said, 'Stefan, Nick is coming back from Mamo's later on, so while I've got you to myself, I will ask you that question once more. Do you really love your family?'

'Yes, I do, I really do.'

He was now feeling hurt that Mor had to ask him again.

'Why, does it mean I ...?'

Mor shook her head.

Stefan knew that meant hush, no more questions allowed. He got out of the car and followed Mor into the house. This time he would be glad to spend the rest of the day reading books on the settee!

Later on that afternoon, Nick came home and afterward Malc. Very soon it was dinner time. Stefan began to wonder again about Mor asking him if he loved his family. Maybe it was something good. If so, what?

Maybe they were going to get a new rabbit. The last one had died. Or perhaps it would be a guinea pig or a cat or even a dog. A dog would be best. He would call it Fred just because it was an easy name to spell. He would get up early on Saturdays and take it for a walk. That would be an important job which he would love to do.

He was still thinking about having a dog when Mor suddenly spoke. 'Now, lads, listen up as we have something to tell you.'

'Yes,' said Malc. 'What do you think about one day having a sister?'

Stefan looked at Nick. Nick was busy drawing squares on the table with his finger. He looked at Mor. She was grinning from ear to ear. Did the grin mean she was going to have a baby?

'Now before you start wondering, it's not a baby, it's a little girl,' continued Malc. 'She hasn't got a mum and dad, and she needs a home. How would you like it if she came to stay with us for a few days so we can get to know her?'

Stefan nodded his head and grinned.

'Does she like spiders?' asked Nick, looking up.

'Well, I don't really know,' said Malc.

'I know where there is one,' said Nick, who got up immediately and ran into the hall.

Just then, the telephone rang.

'Oh, what a time to ring,' said Malc. He got up to answer it, leaving Stefan and Mor still sitting at the table.

'While Malc is away, Stefan, do you remember what I said this afternoon about an important job?'

Stefan nodded.

'Well, this is it. If Bunty—that's her name—does join our family for good, she will go to your school because she's only six. As Nick is going to the big school soon, it would be up to you to look out for her when you can. She won't know anyone. You can be both a brother and a friend to her.'

So that was the important job.

Stefan punched the air.

'Oh, and one last thing,' said Mor. 'The name Bunty means lamb. I just thought you'd like to know.'

And with that, Malc came back into the kitchen.

...

The following week was the school Easter holidays. Stefan, like all the children in The-Front-of-Beyond, heard that the school would reopen after the break. He was glad about that. He even didn't mind seeing Ian Gallice again.

Stefan got better quickly during the following days. He was well enough to go stone skimming with Toby. He was told to wrap up warmly by Mor as it was cold and she didn't want him getting flu. He didn't mind her fussing this time. It was so good to be at home.

Good Friday came, and they all went to church. The Reverend Hard-pew looked different than usual. He smiled a lot. Stefan noticed he looked at Miss Sit-up-straight a lot too. At the beginning of the service, he asked the children to come up to the front. He then asked them why Good Friday was called Good Friday. No one answered. Stefan wondered if, like him, they didn't want to get the answer wrong in front of all the parents.

The Reverend Hard-pew then went on to tell the story of the Last Supper and about Peter who was one of Jesus' disciples. Stefan listened as the Reverend told them how

Jesus said he would be arrested and all the disciples would run away.

Peter said he would never do that, and Jesus said, 'Before the cock crows, you will deny me three times.' That meant Peter would say he didn't know Jesus, and that was what happened. The Reverend Hard-pew said that later on the same day, Jesus was crucified on a cross. Then after three days, Jesus came alive again. So Good Friday is good because Jesus died for all the wrong things we have all done. We have to say sorry, though, so that we can be forgiven.

Stefan listened carefully to the story. He was glad he had said sorry to Jamie, even though Jamie had gone to sleep.

And now he might have a sister sometime in the future. Maybe he could teach her to do stone skimming and climb trees as well as he could.

He liked the idea of his new job. It was better than being a hero.

The End

You can read the story about Peter in the Bible in Luke 22:33–34.
You can read the story of the crucifixion in the Bible in Luke 23: 26–43.
If you want to know what happened after the crucifixion of Jesus, read Luke 24 1–8 in the Bible.
If you want to know what happened to Peter after he denied knowing Jesus, read John 21 1–14 in the Bible.

Finally, these stories that you have read are just pretend. Don't go anywhere without your foster carers or parents knowing where you are. Keep safe.

Also available

THE CHRISTMAS HERO

Anne Jordan

Stefan is worried. Very worried indeed. He loves living in The-Front-of-Beyond, with Mor and Malc and Mamo, and he especially loves Christmas in The-Front-of-Beyond. But this Christmas things may be different. There might be no cheer. There might be no joy. There might be no presents Something is threatening to steal Christmas from the Beyonders. Something bad. And Stefan may be the only one who can stop it.

Anne Jordan lives in Leicestershire with her husband Paul. She has worked as a primary teacher as well as an adult education tutor, teaching people with learning difficulties and disabilities. Anne is now retired but has a heart for vulnerable children as well as a love of history.